"The most beautiful people we have known are those who have known defeat, known suffering, known struggle, known loss, and have found their way out of the depths. These persons have an appreciation, a sensitivity, and an understanding of life that fills them with compassion, gentleness, and a deep loving concern. Beautiful people do not just happen."

Elizabeth Kubler Ross

THE CADUCEAN CHOICE:
A Medical Thriller
By
Douglas Ratner, MD

PROLOGUE

August 20, 2021

Exiting the chartered flight, Dan Marchetti, MD, was struck by the sight of military transports positioned on the tarmac at the airport in Les Cayes, Haiti. The past few days had featured a whirlwind of events which began with the drafting of his resignation letter from Sacred Heart Hospital, a place where he'd practiced his craft for over twenty years. His leadership skills, unflappable nature, and uncanny clinical skills, especially as a diagnostician, was lauded by many. The decision to leave hadn't been made in haste, though the threats on his life and loved ones had inevitably convinced him that no professional ambition was worth such a high price, even for a man for whom "cutting and running" was anathema to every instinct hardwired into his DNA.

Once disembarked, the cool evening breezes of the nearby Caribbean caressed his unshaven face, awakening in him a resurgence of hope. Dan and all the other exhausted volunteer physicians and nurses from all over the United States were led to a makeshift little village, erected by Project Medishare, part of the University of Miami School of Medicine, to help care for the thousands of injured and ailing Haitians left homeless by yet another horrific earthquake.

The Indiana Jones lookalike who'd directed the little city's construction had thought of everything, including portable showers, toilets, and even separate PVC pipes stationed in the ground for the guys to urinate into. In a parcel of land that was a stone's throw from a runway stood three large tents. One housed the roughly one hundred and fifty nurses, X-ray techs, lab assistants, pharmacists, surgeons, internists, and subspecialists, with cots set up in long rows throughout. A second contained a hundred or so more cot beds for medical and surgical patients, its own rudimentary lab with microscopes, a miniature pharmacy with donated medications, a portable chest X-ray machine, and a more diminutive, tented area that served as a de facto emergency room for triaging. Lastly, there was an operating room and surgical ICU, replete with two ventilators, anesthesia apparatuses, and a large area reserved for supplies that had been donated from over seventy countries. It housed everything from ice packs to bottled water and just about any conceivable item in between. But most of all, it offered Dr. Dan Marchetti a haven from certain death at the hands of a brutal criminal underground bent on revenging the loss of their leadership, or so he'd convinced himself.

CHAPTER ONE

Spring, 2004

"Dan, I have some tough news, my friend."

Marchetti barely deciphered his urologist's words as he writhed in pain on the gurney. The previous week had raised all kinds of alarms as the young physician discovered a suspicious lump in his scrotum which proved to be a seminoma, a form of testicular cancer, treatable but necessitating removal of his testes. To make matters worse, a fall he sustained thanks to an uneven sidewalk in front of his condominium had drastically moved up the timetable.

"Dan, both testicles must come out now. I'm so sorry. The torsion from the fall unfortunately has made this a surgical emergency so I'm afraid you will not be able to bank any semen beforehand." The urologist knew that critical time had elapsed for a more hopeful prognosis, as the testicles had been deprived of important blood supply for almost fourteen hours.

"Oh God." Dan barely got the words out. It was like a bad joke: "I have bad news and bad news, you have cancer and, should you survive it, you cannot father children."

When Dr. Comer left to handle an unruly patient in the next room, Dan, now alone, sobbed uncontrollably at the prospect of his impending infertility and potentially life-ending cancer diagnosis. Those last five minutes had shaken the very resilient foundation he always relied upon to get him through the challenges of each day.

The roof seemed to pancake on top of him and the strangest thing happened. Images of past painful encounters with his patients flooded forward until they played on a reverberating loop.

"The news is bad, isn't it?"

"Yes, I'm sorry," Dan told the wife of his first CCU patient as an intern. "Mr. Lawlor has just passed away. I'm so sorry." Like a dark wave, despair overwhelmed him and roiled in the pit of his stomach.

"Thank you for all that you tried to do." A little sob escaped. "I can't believe this. He was smiling and laughing when we left him tonight. Those poor dear boys—" Her voice trailed off.

It was done. Dan rushed to the nearest bathroom and lost his dinner. Shakily, he rinsed his mouth and splashed water on his face. Leaning against the edge of the sink, he stared at himself in the bathroom mirror. His brown eyes had never looked so lost. "I'm not cut out for this shit," he told himself.

Then another. "Sarah! Sarah!" Ed kept pleading. "Oh, God… Bring her back—please!"

Dan closed his eyes to the scene. He motioned all the staff from the room except Wynnie, the charge nurse. Ed Damen deserved at least a moment with his wife. As he left the room, Dan noticed the entire ICU staff peering momentarily at him. A discussion on saddle pulmonary emboli like the one that had just ended his patient's life began among the assembled ICU house staff.

"For God's sake! Would you please stop? A woman just died here."

However, it was not long before Dan received more of his own bad news.

"I can't marry you Dante," Melissa expressed softly, her meek voice cracking. Finally, it was out in the open. Better done now than live a lie one day more. The stress and anguish that had preceded these words had led to abdominal pain and even a loss of hair, she realized.

Dan just stared at his fiancée, or ex, it now appeared, for what seemed an indeterminable amount of time.

"Did I do something terribly wrong? Was I insensitive or too wrapped up in my work?" Dan implored her, diverting his eyes to the ground. "Or is it something more than that?" He closed his eyes tightly as if to ward off any hurtful insight into his personality.

"I love and admire you too much to not honestly explain how I feel, Dan. I want a family and your infertility issue has become a deal-breaker for me." Melissa grimaced at her frivolous choice of words.

Sitting back in the black leather armchair in his living room, the now thoroughly diminished physician blew out all the air in his lungs while clasping his hands behind his head, a habit he'd acquired over the years when contemplating a devastating matter.

The removal of his testes had rendered him without sperm, though the prospect of adoption had always remained a viable option, he believed...

"You hate me, don't you?"

"Hate is a pretty strong word, Melissa. Disappointed in you, rather. I thought our love for each other was mutual... Fuck it! I'm overwhelmed and frankly, just plain wounded, deeply fucking wounded!"

"I'm sorry to hurt you. Best that I get going, I believe."

With those parting words, Dan felt his world disintegrate in front of him. Breaking out into a cold sweat, looking around his apartment, everything seemed so meager and empty despite its spaciousness and new furnishings. Dan knew deep down that if the issue were reversed, it would not have deterred him at all. That reality drove a spear through his now damaged heart.

A personal God, bullshit. There simply can't be.

CHAPTER TWO

For Dominic Antonetti, life had been an interesting journey. Born Christopher Dominic Antonetti (he preferred being called Dominic) to a typical Italian family in Bayonne, New Jersey, he grew up in one of the many row houses with most relatives living close by. A high-school dropout, he traced his hardscrabble life back to a philandering father with matinee idol looks and a resourceful mother who desperately tried to keep together a family of six brothers and sisters.

Dominic found himself making up stories about his absentee father, ever since he could apply his fertile imagination to put imaginary tales together. He was an astronaut away exploring distant galaxies, bringing him home moon rocks (stones taken from his backyard), or a secret agent gone undercover to save the world from foreign bad guys. He would brandish a "silencer," which he constructed from a strange combination of broken plastic containers, attached to a toy pistol, another "gift" from his father. But before long, his friends exposed his stories for what they were, falsehoods conjured up to make himself feel less strange, less abnormal. Then he fabricated stories about his large extended family with grandparents in Europe, aunts and uncles in Italy, and cousins not far from where he lived, the latter at his house almost every day. Before long, his world of imaginary people, jobs, and family became his sole escape from his own dismal reality, full of loneliness and despair.

Being the oldest, Dominic left high school early, rationalizing to make some money for his financially strapped family, though in truth, he wanted to check out from the drudgery of the classroom regardless. He scored a menial job at the local YMCA cleaning bathrooms and showers where he enjoyed free use of the workout facilities, which subsequently became his obsession. As he lifted weights, he stared ceaselessly at his now bulging muscles in the numerous mirrors on the walls. Then came the daily protein shakes, dozens of eggs, endless amounts of chicken and fish, paid for by the money he earned. He had company. The 'Y' had become a real hangout for the two sons of the reputed mob boss Tony "Fats" Soccorso, Alfonso and Tony Jr. The trio became inseparable, Dominic spending so much time at the Soccorso home that their mother routinely set a spot at the dinner table for him. Tony Sr. often referred to him as his third son and, just as he had definitive plans for his own boys in any of several businesses he controlled, he had also begun to plan for his "adopted" son Dominic. Accordingly, he offered the young lad the manager position at the YMCA's juicer bar, which he installed along with more than thirty identical kiosks in numerous locations throughout the county. Permits to operate were either obtained without dissent or through threats of bodily harm. The boy enthusiastically accepted the work, though oblivious to all the behind-the-scenes "negotiations."

Hanging pictures of famous weightlifters on the wall behind the counter suggested that they too drank such products, which was an exaggeration. Nevertheless, the juicer counter became wildly popular, especially among the younger crowd, reportedly making thousands of dollars monthly.

"This kid has a lot of moxie, *cojones*," Soccorso bragged. Finally, Dominic had someone who was proud of his accomplishments, for his own father cared more about himself than anyone else. That major slight aggrieved the young man more than he'd admit. At least this man saw the real worth in him. Before long, he managed five different juicer bars and a vending machine business that brought in a ridiculous amount of cash, most of which went unreported to the IRS. Gradually, the young entrepreneur learned how to fend for himself, though he always felt indebted to the underworld connections of Tony Soccorso. Carrying a gun became a necessity, as well as always wearing a Kevlar vest. It was a life not made for the faint of heart, Dominic thought.

He learned that the bonds within the mafia are sometimes stronger than those found in traditional families, as loyalty and trust run deep among members. At the same time, there also existed a strict hierarchy that offered a sense of structure and order. While the mafia might be steeped in criminal activity and violence, for many like Dominic, it presented a sense of family and belonging that was difficult, if not impossible, for him to find elsewhere, except for perhaps in the military.

However, being part of such a family meant constant awareness of the possibility of being caught by law enforcement or betrayed on occasion by a "family" member. Additionally, *capos* could act out of pure anger or hatred—one didn't need to look any farther than John Gotti himself, who whacked his neighbor for accidentally running over his son when backing out of his driveway.

Yet there was an adrenaline rush that came with being in the mafia. The lure of power, wealth, and control was strong to those who joined. Breaking the law and evading authorities made them feel alive in a way that legitimate careers couldn't offer. This thrill oftentimes led to dangerous and very destructive behavior, with the resulting impact on those around them like family and of course, themselves. Dominic worked hard to sublimate those feelings.

The strict code of conduct and hierarchy of power offered a certain level of mystery and intrigue. For Dominic, the family facilitated the growth of his business enterprises. One could point to his disadvantaged background and lack of a truly loving and cohesive home life and see that he was well-prepped for this life. After passing fifty years of age, he looked back and had no regrets, no regrets at all.

CHAPTER THREE

Dan felt the energy in his body wane after having seen at least thirty-five patients that day.

"Who's my next patient, Maria?" Dan inquired, sneaking a peek at his wristwatch. The long day had begun seven hours ago, with numerous double bookings and same-day visits fit in between regular appointments. "Hope this last one is a cold or something simple and quick."

"Lauren Mason, Doctor."

Dan clicked on the patient's just completed "new patient" questionnaire, hoping to make it a quick turnaround so he could go home already. "Some curious details here," he mouthed to no one as he carefully read the information on her chart. Under the Family History section, there existed no information other than, "No way to know."

Upon completing the form, Dan swirled around on his swivel chair and confronted the new patient just brought in. She was a stunningly beautiful woman with long red hair that flowed down to the middle of her back, a slender build, around five feet eight inches in flats. She wore no makeup except for a light shade of lipstick and possessed a flawless complexion. One eye was brown and one blue, an anomaly for sure, and a first for Dan even after all these years in practice.

"Good afternoon, Lauren, I'm Dr. Marchetti. Welcome."

"Thank you, Doctor. I've heard a lot about you," she replied softly. "I'm a little nervous, I'm afraid, meeting a new internist for the first time."

Dan was impressed that she knew the correct term for physicians who specialize in the internal organs and systems in the body. "Don't be, I don't bite. Let me see, you have a fever up to 102 degrees Fahrenheit, muscle aches, drenching night sweats, and pressure and considerable pain in both cheeks and ears. Correct?"

"Correct."

"How long with these symptoms?"

"On and off for one month."

Dan noted her vital signs were currently good, except for a low-grade fever of 100 degrees (after taking Tylenol), a mild tachycardia, and tenderness over her maxillary sinuses when he tapped over them. Labs were all normal.

"Lauren, I'm going to give you a prescription for Amoxicillin for an infection in your sinuses, a sinusitis. You should do fine."

"Great, I'm going to stay home today and rest. Weekend follows."

"Sounds like a plan. What kind of work are you in?" Dan asked matter-of-factly while he typed in the antibiotic on the computer screen, which immediately uploaded to her pharmacy.

"You won't like my answer." She hesitated but then sheepishly added, "Lawyer."

Dan laughed good-naturedly. "Last I looked, the Hippocratic Oath didn't exclude members of that profession." He paused a moment then added, "Yet."

They both laughed.

"Let me know if you are no better in four or five days or so."

"Will do. Thanks."

Something about her made him think that this issue wouldn't resolve so quickly.

CHAPTER FOUR

Dominic believed he'd discovered some sense of belonging, some meaning to his existence. Then the rug was yanked once again from underneath him. His "adopted" father, Tony Soccorso, was found whacked in the front seat of his Mercedes, his genitalia shoved into his mouth, displacing a lit cigar. The news of the murder devastated Dominic. Once again, he felt alone, abandoned in this world.

Dominic began to pal around with a Jewish boy in town, Jonathan Schwartz, whose father, Marvin Schwartz, had built a construction business from scratch into a multimillion-dollar enterprise, though rumored to be heavily in debt to loan sharks. Possessing a hair-trigger temper and mercurial personality, rumors existed that he'd killed a man with a baseball bat after catching him stealing materials from a particular job for the purpose of reselling on the open market.

Marvin Schwartz possessed a tender side, however, especially when it came to wayward, unloved adolescents, having himself grown up in a home with eight children. Being the second oldest, his parents were too busy and overwhelmed to make him feel particularly treasured. Besides, they were ultra-orthodox Jews who spent a tremendous amount of time observing Jewish rituals and laws. His father avidly studied the Talmud and oftentimes preached, "Make yourself important, because the Talmud says that if you save one man, you save the world." These words resonated with Dominic when he visited the Schwartz home.

One day, Dominic noticed a used CAT pump being thrown out along with other garbage in front of an apartment building near his home. Taking it apart multiple times to see how it worked, he found himself mesmerized by the uniflow design piston pumps with their high-pressure capabilities. Reading avidly about such an engineering marvel, he designed a ceramic plunger pump technology in the late 1970s and early 1980s. Schwartz noted his interest and just like Soccorso before him, recognized his unfailing ambition and decided to front him enough money to convert his tinkering into a true "power-washer" that ultimately cleaned residential and industrial buildings remarkably well.

From there Dominic Antonetti built his business, hiring employees to keep up with the burgeoning demand, averaging one hundred jobs a day. He rented space from Schwartz in an office building he owned downtown, then took some of his profits and plowed his ceramic plunger pumps into the car wash business, which made it more efficient, easier to run, and lastly, more economical, since they required significantly less maintenance. Before long, he had so many orders from other privately owned car washes that he refurbished and outfitted an old tool manufacturing plant in Trenton, New Jersey. At age twenty-four, he'd netted his first of many millions of dollars, to which his benefactor and admirer, Marvin Schwartz, certainly took notice. Before long, his newly expanding business had become a significant contributor to the coffers of the mob and a perfect money-laundering operation. Fortuitously, the mob agreed to forestall any loan repayments in lieu of the income derived from this business.

Still another innovative and highly lucrative scheme was borne out of an article his young wife Abby had shown him regarding the origins of his allergies, which seemed to worsen at home.

"I don't want to read that shit, *bella*."

"Dominic, this article says that many common symptoms we experience come from indoor pollutants and that by making our windows airtight, their levels in our home are higher than outside."

"Whoever wrote that stuff obviously never lived in New Jersey." Dominic smirked but grabbed the article anyway. "I know you'll never leave me alone if I don't read it."

"Thank you." She kissed him on the forehead and left to return to her lasagna preparations. She really was a thoughtful wife, if not a nudge. Truth be told, he craved her attention, the hovering and fussing, more than anyone could know or believe.

He turned his attention to the article.

Biological Contaminants:
Common household biologic contaminants such as bacteria, mold, mildew spores,
viruses, animal dander, cat saliva, mites, cockroaches, pollen, rat and mouse urine can
be distributed throughout the house. They can trigger allergic reactions, runny nose,
asthma exacerbations, pneumonia, and so forth.

Dominic found himself intrigued by the very notion that one's home could render one ill. Low levels of carbon monoxide, nitrogen dioxide, hydrocarbons, certainly radon, formaldehyde, electromagnetic waves, heavy metals, and other pollutants resided there.

It dawned on him that a business of testing, analyzing, and remediation could be developed, and couple that with his real estate enterprises when the findings convinced people to hurriedly sell their homes or buildings. Dominic's company could be there to purchase on the cheap. Especially if bogus claims on the part of his people would scare the owners into selling. It was a dog-eat-dog world out there after all.

Twelve months later, his new company, Environmental Housecall, had gone from six employees to over one-sixty, penetrated twelve state markets, and netted over eighty million dollars per year. Plans to expand nationally were in the works, while the real estate gains were on the ascendency. Testing paraphernalia housed in an indestructible suitcase, accompanying software, and home kits for each homeowner with their own online software option had been developed in record time. Environmental assessment organizations were licensing his materials and promulgating his concepts. Physicians with environmental medicine expertise were put on retainer to add a certain gravitas to the company, while his men used strong-arm techniques to "convince" real estate conglomerates to employ his services.

Not bad for a high school dropout with a troubled childhood.

But now it was time to make healthcare his next cash cow, and why not? It was a four trillion (with a 'T') dollars per year business whose upside was incalculable. Besides, looking at the worst-case scenario, any possible prison time for racketeering would be limited to, at maximum, ten years. Becoming the newest Chairman of the Board at Sacred Heart Hospital represented a brilliant move as now he could maneuver from within to affect his plans.

CHAPTER FIVE

People might have been shocked to learn that an attorney such as Lauren Mason at a large law firm worked anywhere from fifty to sixty hours a week on average, the long hours the result of the obligations the practice of law imposed on them. The image of an attorney heading to court in the morning and spending the remainder of the day engaged in a trial before a panel of jurors or arguing a motion or an appeal in front of a judge is shaped by what people see on television or in the movies, but it's far from the truth.

A typical day in the life of this lawyer was quite varied but usually hectic. Like many attorneys, Lauren wanted to be the first to arrive in the office each morning. Point of fact, her most productive time of the day was the early morning before the offices officially opened for business. The phones were not ringing, clients were not scheduled for appointments, and the other distractions that arose throughout the day were absent. Lauren oftentimes utilized the early hours to catch up on messages and memos from paralegals and other attorneys giving or seeking updates on pending cases.

When her practice did take her to court or to administrative hearings, the hours before the rest of the office staff arrived and before she headed out the door were an excellent time to conduct a last-minute review of the cases on the court docket or hearing calendar for the day.

Lauren's relationships with men also seemed to follow a familiar pattern.

"In love, like, who?"

It didn't take long to realize that something was amiss as this pattern usually played out over a very short amount of time—weeks, as a matter of fact—and not necessarily engineered only by her. She was so hungry to connect with someone, but required frequent reassurance, a malady her therapist coined "anxious attachment style."

In the past few months alone, there had been the refrains:

"Charlie, you say you love me, but I don't even think you like me really."

"When are you going to commit, Brad? It is true that I've only known you six weeks, but..."

"I cooked your dinners for the next six nights because I know how busy you are, Myron."

She'd been attending a lot of expensive therapy sessions to sort it all out. Being born into an unstable childhood can do that to someone, but even so, it was high time to put that anguish behind her, she'd concluded. Thank God for her work, which certainly prevented her thoughts wandering to troublesome areas.

For Lauren, full workdays were no cakewalk. But as of late, there were moments that came at no special time where thoughts of Dr. Dante Marchetti distracted her from her task at hand, no matter how vitally important. This despite him being a man a good twenty years older than her or more. Men her own age disinterested her. Perhaps she'd become fixated on finding a father figure? She hated that hackneyed term, but God only knew her background certainly gave credence to such an observation. The truth was that she found herself strongly drawn to this man, who was also easy on the eyes. Even a hectic calendar like Lauren's proved powerless when confronting matters of the heart.

CHAPTER SIX

Dan decided to drive directly home after leaving his office for the evening. Stopping long enough to get some Indian takeout, his favorite tikka masala and a samosa, he arrived home in time to watch the evening news, inhaling his food concurrently. His thoughts drifted from an update on the war in Ukraine to his flailing love life, or lack thereof. There were times that his infertility made him feel so undesirable and, while he hated to admit it, less masculine. Dan's self-pity party was interrupted by the familiar ringtone of Springsteen's "Born in the USA" on his cell phone. It hadn't been changed for five years as he still was an ardent fan of the Boss, having attended at least half a dozen of his concerts.

"Hi, Mom. How're you feeling?" Gloria Marchetti had been suffering with moderate COPD, caused by years of smoking.

"Better, better, my son, now that I hear your precious voice. I'm more concerned with you, *tesoro*. A man should not be alone. That *ragazza brutissima* years back, that Melissa…"

"Mama, Melissa was being honest, that's all. Better before than after we were married."

"Hadn't she heard of adoption? Besides, good men are hard to come by. Wait until she finds that out."

"Mom, I don't mean to be rude, but I'm tired. Call you this weekend?" Dan needed to get off the phone; the conversation was depressing him even though he knew his mother was just trying to buoy his spirits. A good Italian mother always idolizes their children, especially a firstborn son. And a *dottore*, to boot.

Furthermore, it had been a dozen years since the false accusations made during his residency, where Dan had been accused erroneously of murdering some of his patients, only to be exonerated when the real killers were found. She was still even more protective of him as a result. She was now a widow, her husband Salvatore Marchetti having died a few years back from prostate cancer. The elder Marchetti had been a hard-working laborer whose body simply gave out when he hit his sixties, necessitating his forced retirement. A gentle soul who'd rarely raised his booming voice, he'd enjoyed staying home after work and on weekends, helping his boys with their homework until its complexity overwhelmed him (he'd been a high-school dropout). Sal also had occasionally accompanied his wife Gloria to church on Sunday. The boys had enjoyed kidding him unmercifully, particularly about his expanding waistline. He'd been a slave to his wife's lasagna and *cotoletto Bolognese*, moving his boys on many occasions to declare, "How can someone so round be so square?" They had pretended to box the old man, who resembled a young Jake LaMotta from *Raging Bull*, resulting in the boys laughing hysterically at their dad in a white tee-shirt crouching awkwardly like an old-school prize fighter. His cancer diagnosis had seemed to come from nowhere, and the boys had thought it managed to curtail his life quickly though in reality it took a few years. This was how it was when you loved someone that much.

"*Ti amo, Mama.*" Dante lay down on his futon and stared at the ceiling, his thoughts drifting to his money-making ventures while in medical school. More accurately, money to sustain himself, for his parents were not able to help financially and his bank loans had been maximized.

"Let me see, there was the time I agreed to participate in a drug study along with a dozen other medical students for an unknown pharmaceutical company and felt like shit for nine straight hours, with seventeen blood draws per student." He spoke out loud, shaking his head in disgust at the memory. "Then, the job of all jobs. Jerking off into a CBC tube for artificial insemination, after having been fuckin' hijacked by two OBGYN attendings, partners in a practice, at 2:30 AM while on call. Both men responsible for evaluating my work during the four-week rotation in obstetrics and gynecology. Real ethical! Insemination coercion!" Dan laughed cynically. The irony was that now his own reproductive system couldn't make sperm anymore.

Dan recalled that ridiculous night on call when he'd finally sacked out on the cot the hospital furnished him, at three AM precisely, after having followed a woman in labor all the way to her delivery, a process that had taken twelve agonizing and, yes, tedious hours to play out. Imagine how the mother-to-be felt. After determining that the woman's cervical opening was dilated to eight centimeters, he'd rechecked one hour later to feel with his index finger that the opening had reversed itself to one centimeter.

"That is impossible, son," the attending had told him, and after his own exam, reported back laughing good-naturedly to Dan that the fetus' head was in such a position that the baby was actually sucking on his finger—the rooting reflex. No sooner had Dan placed his exhausted head on the minuscule pillow afforded him (perfect for a microcephalic), than his attending and his partner entered the on-call room, switched on the lights, and pulled up two chairs and placed them by his tired head. No pleasantries, they had gotten right to the point.

"Marchetti, we have a woman coming in at nine AM today for an artificial insemination procedure and we need you to provide a specimen. Of course, you'll be paid for doing so."

Dan had stared at the physician doing the talking, who resembled a young Kris Kristofferson with a full black beard and jet-black hair with just a hint of white around the temples and chin areas.

"Don't you want to know if I carry any genetic abnormalities or inherited disorders?" Dan had replied incredulously.

"Well, do you?"

"Not that I'm aware of."

"Ok, here are two CBC tubes. Collect the specimen here and I will meet you at 8:45 AM, no later, in the hospital lobby. You'll need to repeat the same the next day. We'll pay you $100 each time." With those few presumptuous sentences, they'd departed his tiny sanctuary.

The entire episode had largely been retired to the deep recesses of his mind since then, but now that he was infertile, Dan could not go any appreciable amount of time without acknowledging the nagging feeling that seemed to plague him more often than he cared to admit. That is, hadn't his very essence of 'manliness' been delivered a death blow of sorts? According to the Bible and by Christ's example, masculinity is humble leadership, however. Dan would need to remind himself often of that truth.

CHAPTER SEVEN

"You look like you could do with another drink, my friend." Murphy motioned to the bartender to pour another Jack.

"Thank you. Do I know you?" The glassy-eyed man looked to be in his late thirties, unshaven with greasy, sandy-colored hair, badly in need of shampoo.

"You do now. I'm a friend. Your name?

"Brian, Brian Casey."

"Say, Brian, how would you like to make some easy money?"

Brian rotated ninety degrees on one of the bar's stools. "What are you selling, good sir?" His abrupt shift on the barstool almost deposited him on the concrete-like floor of the tavern.

"Not selling, don't need to sell. Offering."

"Okay, I'll bite. Offering what?"

"Why don't we take our drinks to a table, and I'll describe what I'm referring to?"

With that, both men sought out a location in a secluded area behind a large rectangular planter, Casey trailing behind. At that point the man explained the entire con to his new acquaintance. The scam relied on the well-known Munchausen Syndrome, whose numbers had been on the ascendency nationwide. It was a mental condition with falsified, exaggerated, or self-inflicted physical symptoms.

"The significant rewards would, however, not come right away," he added.

"I see. Now, I don't have a problem with your plan at all, but making money, even large sums in the future, unfortunately won't help me out now. I'm a little down on my luck these days. Could use some real coin now."

A wad of bills appeared before his eyes. "Not a problem, Brian."

Four $100 bills were peeled off and handed to him.

"When do we start?"

CHAPTER EIGHT

"Lauren, I need to ask you some additional questions that could possibly help me figure out what's making you so sick," Marchetti explained while sitting beside her hospital bed. In short order, her illness had worsened despite the antibiotic, necessitating admission to his hospital.

Lauren barely mustered the strength to reply but managed, "Okay. Go ahead."

"Tell me about the health of your parents."

Lauren hesitated before answering, "Now that's going to be a problem."

"How so?"

"Well, for one, my biological father was a sperm donor, a medical student, I was later told by an aunt. And as far as my mother, she died a few years after the birth of my brother and I, and therefore I'm kind of a blank slate. But it's not as if I—we—didn't try to learn more."

"Oh?"

"23 and Me. Sometimes, I'm told, one can find people by registering with them. Anyway, no one came up."

"I see. Well, no matter. Did your mother always live here in Philadelphia?"

"That's my understanding. Why do you ask?"

"No reason. Just curious."

Lauren is twenty-seven, just the right age. Couldn't be, the chances are better to win the lottery. Medical student?

"Let's start at the beginning, Lauren."

"The something-cillin…"

"Amoxicillin."

"Yep—simply didn't make me feel any better at all. In fact, I kept spiking a temperature of 102 degrees, suffered from the worst muscle aches and chills, and at night I was forced to change my pajamas so many times I lost count."

"Why was that?"

"They became drenched. I've never experienced that before, even when I had an occasional fever over the years."

Dan leaned forward in the chair he'd commandeered from the hallway in the Emergency Room so that his face was only a foot away from his patient on the gurney.

"We call them night sweats. Not so uncommon."

"What does that indicate?" Lauren's flushed face grew tense, her eyebrows knitted, her shoulders sagging.

"Not clear yet."

"Still with the pain in both ears and cheeks. Oh, I just remembered—" looking down at her cheat sheet "—I've had double vision on and off for the past two days, and this damn headache." She pointed to both temples.

"I see." Dan continued to write, his concern escalating with this additional history.

Proceeding to examine his clearly ill patient, he took care to press firmly on her scalp. Lauren winced.

"That hurts, a lot, Doctor." Tenderness was also reported when he palpated her jaw and moved her shoulders in different directions. "By the way, I've lost five pounds in the past ten days. No appetite, though."

"Losing one's appetite is very common when you are sick. Excuse me for a minute—I want to look at the lab work I instructed them to take earlier." With that, Dan headed directly for an empty computer station located a few yards from her ER bay.

"Urinalysis is normal, tests for Mono and Tuberculosis are negative, as well as HIV and Lyme disease. Chest X-ray is normal and CAT scan of the sinuses is completely normal," he mused out loud.

Dan sat back in his chair and contemplated his next move. Before long, he was handed a sheet of paper detailing the results of certain inflammatory markers, the sedimentation rate and CRP. Both were markedly elevated, along with a muscle enzyme, aldolase.

"Lauren," Dan called her name gently on his return as his patient had fallen asleep in the interim. It was then that he reflected on her smile as she was abruptly awakened, so reminiscent of his own mother's.

"Must have dozed off."

"Lauren, I looked at your labs and films. I'm going to recommend we obtain a temporal artery biopsy." He touched both to show her where they were located on her skull.

"Okay, I guess. What will that tell you?"

"Well, I need to see if they are inflamed, which would clinch the diagnosis—an entity called Temporal Arteritis."

"Is that serious?"

"Well, insofar as left untreated, it could be. Need to start steroids right now. Can't wait for the results to decide."

"What if you don't start steroids now?"

"You could lose your sight."

With that, his patient burst out crying and shaking. Dan cursed his damn bluntness. He often got so wrapped up in making the diagnosis that he forgot to couch the brutal facts in softer language to make it easier for the patient. Marchetti instinctively gave her a hug and placed his right hand on her shoulder nearest him.

"I'm not going to let that happen, Lauren! Trust me," he whispered.

CHAPTER NINE

"Scott, how are you doing, bud? It's been some time since we last saw each other." Four weeks had elapsed since her discharge from the Sacred Heart Hospital and Lauren had finally regained the strength to go about her usual business. She couldn't help feeling distressed over the scruffy sight of her twin brother. Poor hygiene, scraggly beard, oily hair… not to mention his filthy denim shirt and the beige corduroy pants that had lost most of the cords. Lastly, he also appeared tremendously thin.

"Getting by," he responded unconvincingly.

Lauren sat back in her chair at the local McDonald's, the venue chosen by her fast-food-junkie brother.

"Where are you living?"

"The Y."

"I was lucky I saw you meandering about in town, as otherwise I had no way of reaching you. No phone."

"I know, I know. This nomadic existence will change, you'll see."

"Are you still using?" Lauren's eyes searched her brother's face for the telltale creases and tics that usually revealed when he was openly lying to her.

"You mean, am I self-medicating?" Scott asked rhetorically.

"You could call it that? I prefer to describe it as self-abusing your body."

"Sometimes; I'm trying." Scott paused to take a particularly long drag on his cigarette. "I feel your disgust in me, Lauren."

"Not true. Not true. I love you and want you to be healthy and contented. You and I are basically the only family each of us have. If you were to leave me…" Lauren teared up, though she caught herself. Controlling her emotions had become a necessary talent as it paid dividends in the courtroom, allowing her oratory skills to take front and center.

"Can you even cry, sis?"

"Scott, the truth is… I either don't know how or perhaps refuse to allow my true emotions to show, and because of this 'flaw,' I have very few friends, really."

"I don't know much about that stuff but appearing to always know the correct thing to say, cite an interesting book you just finished, or comment on the latest current event may win you some points in some social circles. But it seems so artificial, so contrived."

"How do you mean?"

"The way I see it, the world is divided between those whose lives seem so perfectly structured—everything in its right place, great career, nice-looking face, pleasing personality—and then there are the others. Meager educations, limited career choices, and, simply put, the 'have-nots,' outliers in this world. The have-nots whose life is one fuckin' struggle. Like mine."

"You want me to pity you? Do you think that would help you?"

"Who said anything about pity? I'm talking about respect, which I don't feel from you."

"When your head is right, you're one of the most amazing and capable human beings I know." Lauren welled up. "Scott, please forgive me. I truly love you."

Maybe this was all he needed. Someone to believe in him. Someone who loved him.

CHAPTER TEN

Russian organized crime, otherwise known as the Russian mafia, the *Bratvia*, originated in the old Soviet Union upon the death of Joseph Stalin. Their honor code became refined after the fall of the Soviet Union, and no less than Louis Freeh, the former director of the FBI, once stated, "The Russian mafia posed the greatest threat to US national security in the mid-1990s." By 2022, the organization remained among the world's largest, deadliest, and most powerful crime syndicates. The FBI description was of a "criminal superpower"—this from a remarkably conservative organization not prone to hyperbole.

The Russian mafia was adept at changing their illegal activities and diversifying into new markets. As criminals from the former Soviet Union became more assimilated into American society, they moved into legitimate businesses such as the textile industry and entertainment, but in many cases these businesses were used for money-laundering. However, an additional characteristic even more definitive of Russian organized crime in the United States was its violence.

"Little Odessa," the group whose home was Brighton Beach, Brooklyn, had developed a unique business acumen: extortion, racketeering, illegal gambling, firearm sales, narcotics trafficking, wire fraud, credit card fraud, identity theft, and now healthcare fraud.

They maintained a loose network structure, unlike the Italian mafia who had their *capofamiglia*, and the Chinese their "mountain masters." However, the Russians had a *Pakhan* or boss who worked through an intermediary, a brigadier, who in turn was watched over by two "spies" who made certain to ensure loyalty. The *shestyorka*, or associates to the organization, were essentially errand boys and represented the lowest rank. They either made it in the organization or were cast aside. Ending up pushed to the sidelines represented a severe blow to their very being, to their self-image in the community, in fact. In essence, the system was set up so that no one became too powerful, and in this important way, they differed from the Italian and Chinese hierarchies.

Dominic Antonetti had become forever indebted to the Russian mafia after they underwrote most of his business entities and schemes. Though he often boasted of fearing no man, truth be told, he feared the Brighton Beach people! Their violent, sadistic acts knew no bounds. This thought occupied his mind when he addressed his associates one afternoon.

"Okay, listen up. As I've been made aware, I have four docs that we know of that have gotten a bit greedy."

His two closest business confidantes listened, knowing that interrupting their boss when he thought out loud usually brought on the "stare." The look that meant that all would be better if they just shut their fuckin' mouths and listened instead.

"A urologist who's deep in debt with us for building a surgical center without other investors. After all, why share the proceeds with others? A gastroenterologist who, believe it or not, is mixed up with an exceptionally vast car theft ring. A doc selling prescriptions for 'oxy' to every fuckoff coming to his practice. I hear they're lining up around the block, and then proceed to sell it on the street for ten times the cost. And lastly, a Jew radiologist who owns his own MRI and CAT scanners and pulls all kind of stunts to cheat the insurers. Men after my own heart, though they need to be reminded who they're indebted to."

He hesitated to look at a text he just received.

"Now, we have to make certain these guys fully understand what we need from their large practices. Medicare numbers and a sizeable piece, say thirty percent of the action. Just the beginning, gentlemen. Healthcare's a potential gold mine. They'll fall in line, just need a little reminding, that's all."

CHAPTER ELEVEN

"John, what do you see?" Dan directed his eyes from the MRI-images to the radiologist reading them. Marchetti had ordered an outpatient MRI on Lauren Mason to study her brain once again, a sign that he still felt uneasy about her precarious state of health.

"Well, Dan, there's considerable expansion of her right cavernous sinus, enhancement of her right middle cranial fossa, as well as meningeal thickening and cord compression at C7-T2. Strange, very strange."

"What do you think?"

"I would tap her spinal fluid."

"Precisely my thought. Will get it down right away." Within twenty-four hours, the fluid was on its way to the lab for analysis, stat. When this physician called, Lauren always made herself available. Such was the enduring faith she held in his clinical judgement.

Opening the computer at one of the desks in his office, a telephone call interrupted Dan's scrolling.

"Dr. Marchetti?" Dan heard the soft, mumbling voice of a woman in her seventies, who sounded as if she had either loose-fitting dentures or quite possibly had had a stroke at some point. "I'm Lauren Mason's aunt, Geri. Do you have any information you can share with me about her?" She inquired timidly.

"Nice to speak with you. She did give me permission to discuss her care with you."

She sounded strangely familiar even with this speech impediment.

"I'm in the process of gathering all pertinent information, but what I can advise you is there's inflammation involving her brain. Whether it's a result of infection, or some other process is still too early to tell. I should have some more information soon that may shed some additional light. But while I have you, Lauren told me of the circumstances surrounding her birth and the tragic death of her mother a few years later, I understand. Her late mother's sister, are you?"

"Yes, yes, I am. The poor thing. She never got a real chance to be the one thing she always wanted to be, a mother. Just a few years, a cruel taste, I'm afraid."

"I'm so sorry. Can I ask you if there were any serious medical diseases in her history, your own, or for that matter your folks?"

"Yes, as a matter of fact, my sister had breathing problems for years and strangely, she was never a smoker."

"A problem with her lungs?" Dan attempted to confirm.

"Yes, some scarring or something. I'm sorry, I'm not sure."

"You're doing just fine. Any name attached to her abnormality?"

"I can't say, I'm sorry. Our parents, on the other hand, died in their eighties of old age."

"I see. Do you know anything about her procedure to get pregnant?"

"Well, nothing more than the daddy was a professional, a doctor in training. She told me that he was pleasant looking with dark hair, Italian."

"Do you know by any chance who the obstetrician was who performed the insemination?" Dan thought he'd take the farfetched chance that she might remember the person from decades ago.

"Can't say that I do, though he had a full head of dark hair and a dark beard with whitish patches, she told me. Very handsome but married." She laughed softly at her wee attempt at humor.

Dan froze, speechless.

Could it be?

***

Dominic Antonetti sat ever so quietly in the back room of the Nelson Gun and Tackle Club savoring the Grappa he so loved, anathema to most. Just the correct amount of grape-based pomace brandy with its thirty-five to sixty percent alcohol by volume, made by distilling the skins, pulp, seeds, and stems left over from winemaking after pressing the grapes. It could only be made in Italy, the Italian part of Switzerland, or in San Marino. The latter was where Dominic imported his ample supply from at home.

He was fifty-five years old now, a sizeable paunch accenting his squat but still imposing weightlifter's build, his regular style of a gold chain necklace and slicked-back black hair aided by transplanted follicles that made up the hairline in front. Not to mention ample amounts of hair dye applied every month.

Being a father had served as a real counterpoint to his dangerous but rewarding business life over the past few decades. Dominic valued immensely the time he spent at home with his children, especially when they were young. The twins, Stacy and Connie, proved to be a handful as they sensed that their identical twin birthright always seemed to attract, almost demand attention when they entered a room. They were stars until their father sat them down one weekend and assured them that they were no more deserving of special attention than their two sisters, Adele and Samantha.

This involved father, sensitive to the fact that his own biologic father rarely showed interest in him growing up, constantly designed activities to share together with all four girls. Building Estes rockets proved to be a popular activity, each daughter given the choice of two rockets from the catalog. Spreading their respective do-it-yourself kits on the large table in the den, their father strode back and forth offering advice on their assemblage but insisting on their completing their tasks on their own. Then when all the rockets were constructed, they'd announce to the neighborhood that a "blast-off" party was scheduled, along with food and other fun activities. All was underwritten by Antonetti himself, which of course added to his soaring popularity in the community.

As they got older, the girls, who were close in age, seemed to need him less and naturally preferred to spend time with their friends. Dating, well, that was a watershed moment. Boys would enter their home shaking and leave even more devastated, according to their daughters' accounts. Just maybe they had good reason, for Dominic knew what was on every boy's mind. After all, he'd lost his virginity at thirteen and would only describe his wanton behavior in those teenage years as "sex crazed."

Regarding their schooling, the girls all attended inordinately expensive private schools, one of the perks derived from his successful business enterprises. Dominic and Abby were committed to them receiving the best education that money could buy.

As difficult as it was to admit it, Dominic still suffered desperately from the unexpected loss of his dear wife, Abby. Unlike other mafia leaders, Dominic had remained faithful to her, as he considered it a sign of total disrespect, a *disgrazia*, to take on a mistress. She had been a dutiful mother to their four daughters every moment of every day, allowing them some freedom to sprout their young wings but not enough to endanger themselves in this increasingly perilous world they inhabited. All four made Dean's Lists and honor rolls and were respectful to their parents and grandparents even as teenagers. But then April 19th came around. A few days after a routine hysterectomy for painful fibroids, a drain was removed and, unbeknownst to her gynecologist, the house staff, nurses, and patient herself, a blood vessel or two ruptured. Soon after arriving home, Abby had gone into cardiac arrest due to catastrophic blood loss. Just like that, Dominic had lost his beloved wife, not due to some nefarious action seen in his world, but by sheer medical incompetence. It was an unusual but not unheard-of complication. The surgical hierarchy had investigated and concluded that the Jackson-Pratt drain, which had been used in surgery for many decades, may have outlived its usefulness owing to its complication rate. Too late for Abby, unfortunately. For Dominic, it represented just one more bump in a road riddled with sizeable potholes and a newfound distrust of surgeons. The "holier-than-thou" healthcare field had its own share of bad actors, despite how they liked to view themselves, he realized.

CHAPTER TWELVE

"You want me to do what?" The diminutive twenty-two-year-old man cried out incredulously.

"A little playacting, that's all. No more peculiar than when you were a kid. Besides, the money will make you a wealthy guy who will only have to work in the future should you want to. Sweet deal, no?" Murphy read his naïve partner-in-crime carefully, noting that his anger had now abruptly dissipated after having digested these last few words.

"Run it by me again," he asked reluctantly.

"I give you these thyroid pills to take, which at worst can make you a little jittery..."

"Jittery, that's it?"

"That's it. You then go to the Emergency Room complaining of feeling 'jumpy,' which will then lead them to treat you."

"Yeah, but how do I—we—make money?"

"They will say you have an overactive thyroid because the lab tests will suggest that possibility, and they will treat you and we sue for malpractice. Since almost all cases are settled because the insurance companies don't want to risk a gigantic lawsuit payout, we all go home elated. Most of all you."

"That simple? What if they figure it out?"

"Only two ways that will happen: if they find the pills on you, which of course they won't, and if they do a thyroid scan."

"A thyroid scan? What's that?"

"Well, they inject some radioactive substance into you. You just let it slip that you're afraid of the damaging effect of the scan, a fear of it causing cancer, and refuse it. Just listen to my advice. You'll do fine."

If they insist, we are shit out of luck. But my guess is they will not. Such is the state of medicine in 2023.

CHAPTER THIRTEEN

March 1996

"Excuse me, you don't know me, and this is kind of awkward and very unprofessional of me…"

Immediately, the woman, who looked to be in her thirties with a peaches-and-cream complexion and wavy auburn hair tied in a ponytail by a teal-colored scrunchie, recoiled. "Who are you?" She asked cautiously.

"I'm a medical student who was asked to donate semen for your artificial insemination procedure. I'm sorry, I don't know your name."

The woman's face turned crimson. "Oh my God. You're the donor?"

"Yes, yes, I was. I can assure you I have a healthy medical record and…"

"That's okay. Actually, I'm relieved to see that you're so nice-looking and have a great smile. The whole process is so strange, the not knowing anything about the 'father' other than you're a medical student, which I must say was reassuring." Just then Samantha "Sam" Mason's unlined but weary face broke out into a wide smile. "Is there something you wish to tell me? I'm sorry, I don't even know your first name."

"Dante—actually Dan."

"For obvious reasons I'm not going to give you my name. I'm sure you can understand, can't you, Dan?"

"Of course! I just wanted you to know that I wish you all the best in the world and that you shouldn't worry about health issues on my side. You see, the whole thing was so impersonal, and I'm a, well… A real person." Dan looked embarrassed to be baring his emotions to a stranger.

"Thank you, that means more than you will ever know." They hugged and Dan left without speaking another word.

Marchetti now turned his attention to his treadmill, which had registered twenty-six minutes at his maximum speed and incline. He wasn't certain why his mind had reverted to that impromptu meeting so many years before, though it gave him great solace thereafter that he'd addressed the anonymity of it all. Dan was sure that the ob-gyn docs were none too delighted about his showing up in person. It was just something he needed to do back then.

CHAPTER FOURTEEN

The two men took turns snorting the coke in front of them, making certain not to waste one iota of the stuff they just scored.

"This con is brilliant, Jimmy. I read the medical record you stole from that patient's chart."

"Which one?"

"The guy with the Goodmaster's Syndrome."

Murphy erupted in cackling laughter. "Goodpasture's Syndrome, you idiot."

"Oh yeah, Goodpasture's. Anyway, let me see if I got this straight. You place an IV in my arm—"

"A PICC line," Murphy corrected.

"I take a syringe and pull out some blood from it, and when I go into the Emergency Room and they ask for a urine sample, I give them one but also empty the contents of the syringe into the open container of pee. Secretly, of course, in the bathroom."

"Correct so far."

"Now, even before that, when they ask me why I came into the Emergency Room in the first place, I answer that I'm told by doctors that I have G-o-o-d-p-a-s-t-u-r-e'-s Syndrome and am experiencing a lot of pain when I pee."

"Doing well. Don't forget to give them the records in this folder."

"Proof that I'm not lying. Correct?"

"Now, when they ask you about what you've been doing the past two years?"

"A Navy pilot. A proud one at that, served with distinction."

"Good. Now, what exposure did you have that could have led to this disease?"

"Jet fuel, according to doctors who specialize in work-related illnesses."

"Right you are. Okay, now when they ask why you have the line in your arm, what do you say?"

"I have been receiving strong medicine through it and have even had a number of procedures where they took blood out and ran it through a machine before returning it to me."

Murphy gave a high five to his new buddy.

"Now, educate me another time on how we make money from all of this." He snorted another line. "Shit, this stuff is good."

Without immediately answering his question, Murphy said, "Now—and this is key—whenever you're questioned, you say 'I believe' I suffer from Goodpasture's Syndrome, which of course you don't. What you really have is something called Munchausen's Syndrome."

"Munch… What the hell is that, *kemosabe?*"

"You're sick in your head and make shit up. After they treat you and do all these things, we then sue the shit out of them for lack of reasonable care."

"You're shitting me. Why would that work?"

"Because ninety-eight percent of all malpractice lawsuits are settled out of court. It simply costs too much in legal fees, etc. to take it all the way to a jury trial. Now, we do this enough times in different hospitals, we can settle back and enjoy our money. Just one catch."

"I knew it. There always is. What is it?"

"Cases don't get settled for at least five years. But at that point, when approached about settling, we agree to the maximum their insurance policy will pay out and no more. Otherwise, the proceedings could go on for years afterwards."

"Well, hell, I can wait. I'm still a young man, only thirty."

"That's right," Murphy responded with a half-smile. What he didn't mention was the damage to one's body by the strong medicines that would be given to him.

This guinea pig will probably never see the bulk of the settlements.

CHAPTER FIFTEEN

"Jeff, here's your plan." Matching up a particular disease with a specific body type was not exactly a science but geared towards the relative IQs of his needy volunteers. This guy was nowhere near as street-savvy as the previous schmuck.

"You go to the hospital's emergency room complaining of the 'worst headache of your life.'" Murphy maintained a serious, contemplative look while instructing his latest pawn in this high-stakes con.

"You clue them in that you get migraines from time to time but this one is so much worse. You effect a limp, pretending to be unable to move your right arm and right leg, and mimic this half-smile that I'm now going to demonstrate." With that, the wily, confident man demonstrated by dragging his leg, holding his arm by his side and half smiling, making certain the mouth on the same side as the leg and arm didn't move.

"They will undoubtedly order CAT scans, MRIs, and probably a slew of other tests to make certain you aren't having a stroke or a bleed in your brain. Certain medicines will be administered and… Bam! We will then allege that they put you in harm's way and failed to diagnose a common migraine with temporary paralysis. It can't miss."

"Will the drugs they give me harm me?"

"Not a bit."

He should have responded with, "They won't harm *me*."

***

The plan was in place. Fifteen men anxious to make some real money, each given a carefully researched list of five hospitals scattered around the United States with horrible records of huge malpractice settlements against their institutions. Three Munchausen case scenarios had been brilliantly constructed to confuse the physicians assigned to their cases and lead them down the road to medical decision-making that put these phony patients needlessly in harm's way. Then they would file suit, because despite their collective and infinite wisdom, the physicians would fail to figure out the charade. Now, it was true that collateral damage might and probably would occur for his cadre of misfits but still, how else could these unfortunates get by except with a "helping hand' from a benefactor like himself?

Besides, the medical profession had missed his own diagnosis of overwhelming sepsis that had led to the horrendous amputation of both feet and the fingertips of all ten digits. Necrotizing fasciitis they later called it, the so-called "flesh-eating" infection that is usually deadly.

They should have let me die rather than trying to navigate through life as a freak. Not to worry, their comeuppance was on the way.

Murphy also took abundant care not to allow any of his 'disciples' to know his identity or how to implicate him in any of these scenarios. Besides, who would believe any of these individuals' accounts, with their dubious histories of theft, prevarications, and marked criminal backgrounds?

He was a patient man, and it didn't bother him in the least that settlements in these kinds of lawsuits took on average three to five years. But when they came, they would come in bunches. Kinda like bluefishing. He remembered when fishing on a party boat with his dad that when the Captain located on his finder a school of blues, as many as eight or so individuals could be battling a nice size blue all at exactly the same time! Now that was fun.

CHAPTER SIXTEEN

Dominic Antonetti had just finished looking at the baseball box scores from the night before. His long-time favorite team since the days of 'The Mick', the New York Yankees, had just completed a day-night doubleheader sweep. These victories lengthened an already large lead in their division over his despised Boston Red Sox. Finishing his second cup of espresso with a hint of grappa, he was ready to take on his day. Unlike the image the public still had of made men like Gotti or Gambino, the "Executive" had positioned his family years before to infiltrate the most lucrative business of them all, the healthcare industry. This four-trillion-dollar-a-year business had stimulated his interest for a long time, and for obvious reasons. It was rife with tremendous inefficiencies and what he perceived were golden opportunities for scamming and subterfuge. Take the Medicare fraud racket, for example. There were always superior opportunities when compared to protection schemes, loansharking, drug-dealing, or robberies. Recruiting shady physicians and willing patients was a relatively smooth operation. Medicare alone could bring in hundreds of thousands daily which, if scaled correctly with proper management, could easily quadruple the take. Sure, he'd be eligible for Medicare benefits the following year and why not? What did one thing have to do with another?

"Boss, what's on your mind?" Asked Salvatore Trombino, one of his lieutenants, who sat across from him that morning at the famous Frick N' Frack Diner in Rutherford, New Jersey.

"Been thinking about another business idea. There are many health service companies owed a great deal of money by hospitals. We buy up the invoices at a discount and then package them into a much larger pool of invoices, then in turn sell bonds to investors backed by the invoices. The investors then earn interest on the bonds as the invoices are gradually paid off."

"I get it. No different than debt instruments using certain financial engineering like we see done all the time by hedge funds and various investment banks." Trombino had an MBA from Seton Hall and represented the new up and coming racketeers entering the mafia ranks.

"Also, I've learned about some smalltime outfit trying to shake down many hospitals by filing bogus lawsuits. They're counting on the lawyers and insurers almost always deciding to settle rather than risk large, damaging judgements."

"Okay. I'm listening."

"We agree to make these lawsuits disappear for the hospitals in exchange for certain inducements."

"Such as?"

"Learning about the sicker patients who we can sell our funeral services to and a list of other benefits that would accrue to our bottom line. Not to mention gaining access to databases with Medicare numbers and the like. The take would be astronomical."

It's time we grow our businesses using the healthcare world as our own ATM.

CHAPTER SEVENTEEN

Dan went about his usual weekend chores, having just completed his rounds at the hospital that morning. Shoving his dirty laundry into the washing machine was high on his to-do list. Not far from his thoughts was the nagging possibility, however remote, that his patient, Lauren Mason, had been the result of his having donated semen back in medical school. The description of the fertility doctor, the timing, the Philadelphia area raised the possibility, but most suggestive were the facial expressions. They mirrored his own, he thought, as he poured the detergent into that damned tiny pull-out drawer in his washing machine.

23 and me—it was worth the few dollars to see if a match came up. After all, she'd mentioned that she had sent in her sample to the same company to locate her biological father but to no avail. She was in the system.

He'd already tracked down Dr. Napier, the physician who had coerced the semen donation from him twenty-seven years before. He was due to retire in six months, but it had been worth the visit which Dan had carried out the day before.

"Dr. Napier, my name is Dan Marchetti, an internist in town. I don't expect you to remember me…"

"Dan, I may be getting old, but I am not demented yet. Your name sounds familiar," he had responded good-naturedly. Dan had been certain that Napier was just being polite.

"Well, you precepted me during a third-year ob-gyn rotation in medical school."

"I see, I see. How can I help you?"

"Well, I participated in an artificial insemination procedure you performed twenty-seven years ago and…"

"Wait just a minute. I don't want to entangle myself in any litigation, especially this close to my retirement. God knows, we docs get sued enough and I am no exception."

"No, no, nothing like that. I have a patient whose age and geographic placement match up and, damn, she bears an uncanny resemblance. Anyway, she's very ill as we speak, and I have no genetic background at all which could shed light on her condition."

Better keep this totally medical if there is any chance Napier would talk freely.

"Son, do you have any idea the hundreds of inseminations that I performed over the years?"

"I'm sure."

"Frankly, I doubt very much I put down in the chart where I received the specimen. Anonymous, you know. Besides, in some cases," he'd leaned forward and lowered his gravelly voice, "when I ran up against it, I myself volunteered, though if anyone should ask, I would deny this fact one-hundred percent."

"Thank you for your time. So, if I hear you correctly, you never wrote down anything about the donors?"

"Rarely—very few."

"Well, if you get a chance, the surname for the woman is Mason." Dan had turned on his heels and left. Frankly, there had been something disturbing about this man, then and now. The part about his furnishing his own semen at times had seemed very unethical and could very well have been much more than a few. In fact, every few years there appeared in the news some obstetrician fathering hundreds of children born from mothers in their practices.

Oh, what a tangled web we weave.

Driving back to his office that frigid Wednesday morning, Dan couldn't help but notice the gaggle of reporters milling about in front of the county courthouse. He became gripped by the disturbing memory of when his freedom was placed in serious jeopardy for a series of crimes he never committed as an intern. Eventually exonerated, some enterprising journalist had named the proceedings then as the "trial of the decade." Dan gripped the steering wheel until his fingers turned white.

"The Commonwealth of Pennsylvania," a booming voice broke through the buzz, "versus Dante Michael Marchetti."

Dan's eyes snapped open, as if surprised to see a courtroom. How was it that he was here, on trial, indicted for murdering his patients? He was a doctor, not a danger; it was his job to save people's lives, damn it. How could anyone think otherwise—that he'd willfully kill patients?

"I'm innocent, God damn it to hell!" He screamed at the top of his lungs.

CHAPTER EIGHTEEN

"I'm looking for my brother, Scott Mason. Is he still staying here at the Y?" Lauren looked intently at the young woman behind the registration desk. She still felt moderately weak after her stay in the hospital.

"Let me see. Yes, he is. I'll ring his room for you. And who shall I say is asking for him?" The pimply-faced teenager earnestly inquired.

"His sister Lauren."

After waiting a few moments, Scott answered the phone in his room, only to notify his concerned sister that he was too sick to come down.

"Which room is his?" Lauren turned to the teenager after Scott abruptly hung up on her.

"424, but I can't let…"

Lauren didn't wait for the clerk's warning, having accessed the stairs and slowly navigated each step to Scott's floor. The hallways were in dire need of a fresh coat of paint; his room was the last one on the northwest side of the building. Lauren knocked firmly and repeatedly until she heard her brother yell, "Go away, Lauren! Another time."

"Scotty, open the door. I have to talk with you. It's important!" Lauren heard the hellish coughing and rattling in his chest through the metallic door. "I want to help, please."

Moments went by, but slowly he approached the door and removed the chain that he believed kept him safe. Peeking through the narrow crack, Lauren was aghast at the sight of her brother, who had seemingly aged immeasurably since she saw him that morning at McDonald's a while back. His eyes were sunken, his hair matted down with perspiration, and his skin color a sickly yellow-green. A handkerchief was in his right hand while his left covered his mouth as he tried vainly to suppress a cough.

"Scotty, for God's sake, you're very sick, let me take you to the hospital."

Before he could respond, Lauren heard a loud thump, only to see her brother's head hit the rigid floor and let go a loud groan before losing consciousness. Within moments, she had called 911 and had placed a rolled-up pillowcase under his head, now bleeding profusely from a sizeable gash on the side.

The simple truth was that her brother's life had been an unmitigated disaster to date. But he was still her brother, her own flesh and blood.

CHAPTER NINETEEN

"Dr. Marchetti, I'm sorry to barge into your office during your office hours, but I desperately need your help regarding my brother Scott, who I brought to Sacred Heart's Emergency Room fifteen minutes ago. He's quite sick, I'm afraid, but to look at him, you're probably going to think the worst about him. But he's not a bum, despite how he might appear on the outside. Fallen on some tough times, I'm afraid." At that moment, Maria came charging in, having tried to stop Lauren in the waiting room but to no avail.

"Dr. Marchetti, she wouldn't stop…"

"It's okay, I have a few minutes." Dan gave an understanding nod to Lauren. "Tell me more about your brother Scott. No judgements here." He touched her shoulder.

"Thank you. Where should I start?"

"You say he's experienced a hard life. How so?"

"Well, ever since he was a child, his behavior was off, I mean way off. My aunt at times felt overmatched, his getting in trouble at school, displaying a horrible temper, fighting, screaming at her, at me…" Her voice trailed off noticeably.

Dan listened attentively, not interrupting at all.

"He went to five schools before barely graduating high school. Few friends. He became accustomed to entertaining himself with K'NEX toys, puzzles, and the like. I'm afraid I wasn't there for him much. Had my own issues to deal with."

"What were they?" Dan leaned forward, his large brown eyes now glistening.

"Well, no real parents, an aunt constantly distracted, mostly disinterested, not a very good listener and often inebriated… Looking around at all those 'complete' families, I was so envious and oh so angry, spent a lotta time feeling sorry for myself and my brother." Lauren let out a protracted sigh.

"I'm so sorry, it's heartbreaking really." Dan hesitated to contemplate his next question. "But look at you, at what you've become, a practicing lawyer. That couldn't have been a snap. And Scott?"

"Became a valuable member of the SEAL Team Six after a high-school teacher straightened him out, graduating him. Smart guy."

"A teacher took interest in him?"

"Yes, from one of those state-funded schools for children like Scott. This teacher owned the school but in his earlier life, he'd been a physical education teacher who also coached wrestling. One day, when Scott had been acting out, he body-slammed him against the wall, uttered some choice words, and ever since that day, Scott toed the line. They stayed in touch for a long time."

"Then what transpired to lead to his present difficulties…?"

"Scott received significant shrapnel wounds in Yemen, couldn't seem to get his bearings when he returned to civilian life after, I believe, eight years in special forces. Been in trouble with the law, addicted to meth and heroin, in and out of serious predicaments of his own doing, I'm afraid."

Dan just listened intently. Her words really mattered to him.

"I see how much you love him."

"He's the only real family I have." She looked at her physician pleadingly. "Would you do me a huge favor and agree to take care of Scott?" Lauren put her hand over her mouth momentarily before observing, "I just came from the ER, there were wall-to-wall patients, many lining the hallways."

"Sure thing. I'm finishing up my office hours and will head right over. In the meantime, I'll look at his chart online. His full name is Scott Ma…son?" He froze, the twin brother… The names of the children he helped conceive with his semen were different, though their initials were the same. How strange. Could they be one and the same?

Can't be.

His mind seemed poised to believe something that on the surface seemed preposterous and highly improbable.

Did the aunt change the names, move away, and then move back?
***

Lauren waited anxiously in a chair by her brother's gurney for Dan's arrival, with a combination of worry for his wellbeing and some embarrassment for his unkempt appearance and poor station in life.

Scott's devolving into the world of addiction had been extremely difficult to accept, even though she knew inherently it was considered a disease like many others.

A hand gently gripped her right shoulder; it belonged to Dan Marchetti.

Lauren placed her hand on his, the spontaneous touching abruptly interrupted by a violent coughing spell from the patient himself.

"Hello, Scott."

"What is it?" Scott spoke angrily, not even bothering to look in the direction of the voice.

"Scott, Dr. Marchetti's here to help. Don't speak to him that way, even if you're not feeling well."

"Lauren, can I speak to you outside for a minute?" Dan suggested in a soft voice.

"Okay." Lauren followed Dan outside the immediate area, out of hearing range of her ailing brother.

"Lauren, your brother and I know each other. I've treated him in the past and have had to talk with him firmly about his using. I told him that these drugs were going to kill him without any doubt whatsoever, and sooner rather than later."

"I see," she responded dejectedly.

Dan sensed her sinking into a sullen mood.

"He sounds like he has pneumonia, or possibly TB with that cough. I think it better to find someone new to treat him. Agreed?"

"I do. Please choose someone as capable as you."

"You have my word." They hugged briefly.

Maybe if I circle back and really have a heart to heart, it would help, Dan thought.

CHAPTER TWENTY

"Scott, a Dr. Jacob Weiner, an excellent doctor, is going to try hard to get you better, but using is going to kill you as sure as I'm standing here right now." Dan felt protective of Lauren's twin brother, now under the care of a capable colleague.

The intravenous drugs had led to a diagnosis of endocarditis, a serious infection involving one of Scott's heart valves. If left untreated, without antibiotics and perhaps surgery, the infection would eventually erode the valve until death occurred or overwhelming infection intervened.

"Why bother? My life has been in the shitter for quite a while." The despondent look on the young man's handsome but now sickly face affected Dan Marchetti to his very core.

Why this man? Hadn't he seen scores of men and women exhibiting this state of mind over the years?

But Dan couldn't shake the ominous and disquieting feeling reaching out to his inner soul.

"I want to know more about you." With that, Marchetti sat down, crossed his legs, and settled in for an honest discussion.

"I'm sure you have more important things to do than listen to my sorry story." Scott looked away, embarrassed by the attention given him just then, and frankly sensing perhaps a pretense of concern to win points with his sister.

"Nope, not one thing better." Dan smiled reassuringly, his genuine sincerity hard for Scott to misinterpret, if he allowed himself.

"Okay, I spent eight years in special forces, SEAL Team Six."

Though Dan knew this, he sat up straight with both feet now firmly planted on the ground, wanting to give Scott his just due. "That is some accomplishment, and let me say, thank you for your service. God that's impressive," he exclaimed.

Scott felt an overwhelming surge of pride course through his body as someone saw him for who he'd been, as opposed to a deadbeat crackhead, a non-contributor to society. Managing a weak smile, Scott continued, "Seeking to be a member of such an elite force was not a decision one took lightly."

Dan nodded his head in agreement. "Not unlike the field of medicine, I imagine, but significantly more dangerous."

"I suppose, but the comical thing is that the training is so intense and so monumentally difficult that they make you feel that you have the tools to survive just about anything."

Dan saw the intensity return to this lost man's eyes. "There are very few men and women now, I think, who could withstand the physical and mental rigors that I'm certain are just partially known to those of us not in that special, rarefied club. Scott, when and where did you go temporarily, and I mean that—temporarily—off the tracks?"

"The day I arrived home from deployment… Couldn't handle the transition from going a hundred miles per hour to zero, or so it seemed. Does that make sense?" He asked rhetorically, not really needing an answer. "What was wrong with me?" He paused for a second. "There were the wounds, several of them. I was given meds, oxy and stuff… Well, you know how that ends up, I'm sure."

"I do," Dan added, more interested in listening than adding his two cents.

"Then…" Scott sobbed openly, unashamedly. "…Then, one by one, my buddies offed themselves, one after another. The last one was my commanding officer, Captain Jack Barnes, the one who we all looked up to, the one who appeared to have everything working for him, everything figured out." His voice trailed off. "His shit together," he whispered. Scott stared at Marchetti for a protracted moment, as if he was waiting for some kind of answer that would make all the pain go away.

Sensing the opening, Dan leaned forward. "You know, I'm a movie buff and I remember an old movie called *La Dolce Vita*, a Fellini movie, a famous Italian director, that is. Anyway, this character Marcello, a gossip reporter of sorts, who spends his waking days and nights in pursuit of celebrity scoops to report on as well as meaningless, silly pleasures, discovers that one of his friends, who he believed to have achieved a real life of meaning, has suddenly killed himself. Well, his only hope for some coherence, some value to this life we are given, was shattered instantly."

Dan gathered his words carefully before proceeding, while his audience sat in rapt attention. "There is Scott the self we want everyone to see and then there is the 'true' self, your private self, which we shield. This is normal, but a fluid channel of communication between the two must remain open. Without that, according to British psychiatrist R. D. Laing, 'we run the risk of being torn apart.'"

"I don't understand…"

"With you Scott, I suspect that, on one level, the adrenaline surge you received in the special forces, which had been turned on for eight years in Afghanistan, Yemen, or other dangerous places, didn't automatically shut off when you returned home. A well-known phenomenon, I'm told. I believe the loss you and your sister felt so early in childhood and I believe till this very day has plagued you additionally. Now, though you only had a few years with your loving mother, you have to know that she carried a deep love for you both that needs to sustain you. As far as a father goes, I'm certain that your biologic father would be so proud to call you both his children if the arrangement had been a different one. I know I would! Please know that losing a parent during childhood can create a lasting fear of abandonment, 'abandonment trauma,' it is called. Heh, if your true self stays in touch with your external self, you'll understand why certain emotions and actions seem to occur. Only then, can you evaluate, recalibrate, and go on. We all need to do just that!" At that moment, Marchetti's beeper went off, directing him to another floor of the hospital.

After the doctor had gone, the ex-SEAL recalled the time in fourth-grade art class when the students were instructed to design Father's Day cards. When he approached the teacher to inform her that he didn't have a father, she then proceeded very softly to request he draw a Mother's Day card instead. Scott was too ashamed to tell her that he came up zero on that one too, so he pretended.

As Dan hurried to his next patient, he reflected that he had been glad to use that excuse to leave his words to resonate and not to overstay his welcome.

The words applied to himself as well.

Meanwhile, Scott contemplated the significance of the past thirty minutes. For the first time in a very long time, a smile appeared on his unshaven face.

He knew that Lauren certainly deserved to have someone special in her life after all this time. To meet someone of some worth, someone who would treat her with respect, compassion, and, yes, love. She seemed to find guys that treated her in the shameful way many men can: abusively, unfaithfully, and the like. Now, he would have to be blind to not notice the undercurrents of something. This amount of care afforded both affected this decorated soldier as if a seismic weight had been lifted off his chest, allowing him to breathe freely.

CHAPTER TWENTY-ONE

James "Jimbo" Faulkner woke from his drunken stupor by a loud banging on his apartment door. He'd passed out from his sloppy binge in the early morning hours and found himself on his threadbare couch with the TV on and his rescue dog, Petey, snuggled up against him. Fritos corn chips, some broken and some still whole, lay scattered on his sweat-stained tee-shirt, while his laptop had long since timed out from his last event of the morning, pleasuring himself to his favorite porn, MILFS.

"Be right there." He spoke quietly, as any significant noise threatened to pound his aching head into utter despair. Jimbo had even forgotten to latch the entrance as was his custom before retiring for the night, an observation that caused him to scowl at his carelessness after the first two six-packs of Bud. They'd caused him to not exercise his usual caution, for he knew of several characters who wished him no good.

Opening the door a crack, Jimbo found himself knocked over by the force of the metal structure and looking up at two men he'd never met.

"What the fuck! Who…"

Before he could even finish the sentence, one burly guy who stood at least six feet and a half had grabbed him by his long, stringy hair and literally heaved his body onto his sofa, which doubled as his bed. The other, short and dumpy, a Clemenza clone from *The Godfather*, spoke with a strange high-pitched voice, "James Faulkner?"

"Yeah, that's right. Who's asking?"

Clemenza-lite took the remote and turned the volume up while the other man pummeled Faulkner's face repeatedly until it became a bloody, pulpy mess. Petey barked loudly and repeatedly but was reduced to a whimpering mess after sustaining a swift kick from the burly man's work boot to his midsection. Just before losing consciousness, his master managed to hear these words:

"That lawsuit you're involved in against the Sacred Heart Hospital in New Jersey. You will refuse to participate, or else my friend and I will return to finish the job. You must realize that a few more blows to your body, properly placed, will end your life for certain, or at least make your every waking moment worse than death itself. Am I understood, my good friend?"

Jimbo tried to speak, but even simply uttering, "I understand" proved too painful, since some of his now broken teeth had embedded in his upper lip. Instead, he managed an excruciating nod of his head.

Both men responded in unison, "Good."

With that they exited the apartment to finish additional assignments elsewhere. They had a full workload that day.

CHAPTER TWENTY-TWO

Martin "Marty" Forsythe, recently promoted to the head of New York's FBI office, remembered years before listening to Dr. David Kessler, the former Commissioner of the US Food and Drug administration, describe his first day as head of the FDA. One of the senior officers there approached him on day one with, "Let's go after the tobacco industry," one of, if not the most powerful lobbies in the country. After being momentarily shocked by the request so soon after taking over, he finally warmed to the idea and did just that. Though unsuccessful at first, his people ultimately prevailed, not before suffering the slings and arrows from the powerful tobacco industry.

Forsythe possessed the same ambitious streak, aware that significant political capital is automatically assigned to someone who ascends to a position of power, initially, that is. Kessler's pursuit of the tobacco industry would be analogous to Forsythe's examination of the underworld's infiltration into healthcare, especially in the tri-state region. The amount of Medicare fraud had grown exponentially, with all kinds of angles invented to allow for access to their billing systems, such as infiltrating union plans, aligning with palliative care efforts to siphon off donations, coopting lucrative funeral industry contracts, and so forth.

The latest, however—preventing scam malpractice suits before a jury is allowed to compensate the aggrieved party—didn't make any sense, at least on the surface. This one had just appeared on their radar thanks to an alert from their Trenton office, where a plaintiff in a malpractice suit was viciously and savagely beaten to dissuade any further action against a hospital being targeted. This strong-arm tactic seemed to represent some vendetta or internecine battle among the families. Whatever the rationale for such behavior, Forsythe knew that the motives were suspect for certain. Mobsters always had an angle.

CHAPTER TWENTY-THREE

Dan sat on the park bench, raised his exhausted and sleep-deprived head, and stared at the blackened sky to observe the full moon. As a child, he'd deciphered its 'face' and imagined all the possible images: a baseball field, the Statue of Liberty, a piece of Swiss cheese… Now he deciphered only a handgun in the shape of the one Alex Cole brandished that fateful day in his apartment years back, soon after Marchetti had discovered the correspondence Vinny Orlander had sent him detailing his heinous participation in the killings that he, Dante Marchetti, never committed but stood trial for. The letter had read:

> *Dr. Cole,*
> *Welcome back. As you know, I followed through on your suggestions and arranged for a few early "departures" for Marchetti's patients. After all, he needed to be taken down a few pegs, and they were terminal patients anyway. Certainly, the actions dimmed our illustrious doctor's star and made him appear more like the rest of us. His arrest, I suppose, was what the military deem, "collateral damage." However, I must confess that the act of taking a person's life can get addictive and even, I dare say, intoxicating. Hence, Trey Hartman, Dr. Ballard, and even Matt Saxon. I believe you'll cut me some slack here. As my grandmother often remarked (translated to English), "We're cut from the same cloth."*
> *Your friend,*
> *Vinny*

"Alex, is this what I think it is?" Dante had said.

"Yes. Your ticket to freedom, you lucky guy!" He retrieved a 9mm Springfield XD-M Elite model handgun from behind a large, empty, deep-blue vase on the bookshelf. Pointing it at the side of his head, he continued, "And my reason to exit this wonderful world we live in. Oh yes, Alex Cole has so much to be proud of and thankful for," he uttered mockingly. "It was in my mailbox yesterday." Pointing at the letter, he added, "Another sick fuck, huh? I posted a copy of the letter to the prosecutor's office earlier today, along with my own part in this whole mess. You'll be completely exonerated." He paused and added, "I'm the one who caused all your problems. As you can see, I told that schmuck Vinny Orlander we should take you down a peg or so. It was my idea for him to fix it so some of your patients checked out a little early." Alex stared at the ground, girding himself for the outrage, the condemnation. "The fucker ran with it…"

"What? For what reason?"

"Isn't it obvious? I'm so fuckin' envious of you. All the accolades from the attendings and all the attention. Jeez, you'd think you walk on fuckin' water. Orlander fiddled with ventilator settings, Sengstaken-Blakemore tubes, damaged a lead wire on an EKG, released mast trouser valves… All those patients were gonna die anyway, but he—we—helped them along. As you can see, though, he did the baseball player on his own, Ballard, and even Matt Saxon. And that poor bastard Lloyd Smith—wrong place, wrong time."

"Lloyd Smith? The nitrous oxide overdose?" Dan hesitated to make sense of it all. "Why in God's name would envy lead you to such heinous acts? You were well on your way. Wasn't that enough?"

"You know, I've asked myself that same question so many times. I've worked so hard to succeed, but not because I wanted to be the best doctor for my patients. Not at all. I worked so fuckin' hard because I wanted all the kudos, the esteem, the God complex, all of it. You see, I've been in it for all the wrong reasons!" Cole's face was a crimson red by now from embarrassment and utter shame.

By making me look bad, thought Dan. *Depraved.*

Alex regained his composure. "I tried to end this pitiful life once before, but you saved me. Dante to the rescue once again," he announced sarcastically. He took a little cassette recorder from his jacket, turned it off, and placed it on the coffee table next to him. Without hesitating at all, he placed the gun barrel inside his mouth and discharged it.

CHAPTER TWENTY-FOUR

Dan rifled through the mail in his office, anxious to finish the sorting so that he could conclude his workday finally. 8 PM and he still hadn't eaten dinner; his last meal was a ham and cheese sandwich he wolfed down at 1 PM.

At once, his pulse quickened when he glimpsed a return address that read, "23 and Me."

No DNA matches noted from our database.

So that issue was settled. Dan didn't know if this information was a relief or a disappointment, especially considering his own infertility. But peace of mind was worth something, and it was the not knowing that truly caused his uneasiness, even restlessness.

Dan ruminated on what he said to Scott, that in essence whatever is visible in a person's external personality is an indication that the exact opposite resides in the shadow. Stoical versus emotional, 'tough as nails' or fearful, acerbic or tender, cheerful or wistful, self-sacrificing or selfish, needy or independent, and so on. Take Lauren and her physical beauty, which, she confided to him in a rare moment of reflection, seemed to attract the 'wrong' kind of attention. She therefore focused on blending in and purposefully played down her physical attractiveness, allowing it to recede to the shadow. Additionally, Lauren was determined to mostly conduct herself in a respectful manner but occasionally would permit anger to break through, staying in touch with her inner self. She herself was aware that she'd relegated unbridled rage to be forever hidden in the shadows. Very often, we identify with our conscious personalities, though again, everything we stuff into the shadows are still a *part* of us. Knowing when to reclaim those parts into our conscious behavior and into the light prevents them from causing the exercising of unconscious impulses. For Dan himself, allowing for his show of emotions, his fear to occasionally surface, his tenderness to prevail, while displaying gloom and occasional selfishness, seemed to prevent inappropriate reactions to constantly surface.

Made sense in theory, anyway.

CHAPTER TWENTY-FIVE

"Lauren, how are you feeling on the new meds?" Dan sat back in his office chair and unfastened the top button of his shirt while simultaneously loosening his tie.

"Why do you guys wear those things, they look so uncomfortable? The image, huh?"

"Nah, habit." With that, Marchetti ripped off the dark blue striped number and undid one more button. "How's that?"

"Much better. Must feel good, huh?"

"Back to you."

"Okay,   would you believe it—what you guys call 'asymptomatic.' No complaints whatsoever." Lauren lost eye contact, her cheeks reddening. "I owe you my life, and I mean that from the bottom of my very being."

Dan brushed away her words, always uncomfortable in fielding a compliment or receiving a heartfelt thank you.

"So, what's your to-do list now? Back to work? Vacation time?"

"Well, the firm has a lot of lawyers and I have a good deal of vacation time, personal days, sick time… Thought of taking a cruise."

"Sounds great. I'm envious. Someplace warm, I hope."

"Haven't gotten to that decision yet. When was the last time you took some real time off?"

Dan ran his fingers through his hair before cupping them behind his head and gazing at the ceiling. "Couldn't even tell you. How pathetic."

"I have an idea. Why don't you join me?"

"I'm afraid that would be simply impossible. I am still your doctor, though you are to follow with the rheumatologist. Maybe we can grab a bite together instead?"

***

"It's been quite some time since I have been out on the town, I'm afraid. Little out of practice," Dan stated sheepishly.

Lauren smiled back reassuringly. "You're fine. Why haven't you ventured out much? Good-looking guy, a professional, kind eyes…"

"I could say my work occupies so much of my time, but that would be only slightly true. A trust thing, I'm embarrassed to say, especially at my age."

But you agreed to go on a cruise with me?

"Really, frankly it's a bit surprising, I guess. You're safe, you see. Our age difference, to my way of thinking, makes you a friend, a younger one at that, but someone who's relatable. Different expectations for the future, life experiences, power dynamics, and so many more reasons why anything more would be doomed to failure."

"Having my life saved by you essentially is an incredibly persuasive pull. Thank you."

"I thought of that possibility."

"It's a good thing, in my opinion, comes from tremendous respect for your abilities and the warmth and caring you give off."

Dan smiled. "Sometimes, though, the light you believe you are giving off is not the same as what people are seeing. And of course, there's the pain we carry within."

"What pain are you carrying, Dan? What shuts you down?"

He decided to address her question with one of his own. "When you were choosing me as your doctor, I assume you Googled me?"

"I did."

"And…"

"It gave me pause, to be honest, but when I asked around, I found your reputation to be outstanding. Decided to trust my gut. Besides, you were Harrison Ford in *The Fugitive*."

"I guess if I'm to be compared to a movie star, he's not a bad one to be identified with." They both grinned. "You asked about getting 'shut down.' My response, uncertainties, the vagaries in life. Being erroneously tried for murder can do that to someone. Never in a million years did I ever imagine that happening to me."

Lauren placed her hand on his and whispered, "We're all wounded birds, Dan, we fly higher and farther depending on how much nurturing we've received. Believe me, I know a good deal about this." She let out a big sigh. "There can be unpredictable responses from others, at times generous, but many more times, cruel and selfish. I figure they're fighting their own demons."

Dante shook his head in agreement.

Tears streamed down both Lauren's flushed cheeks while her nose dripped. "Look at this, a real mess." They both laughed.

"Don and Debbie Downers." Dan waved a dismissive hand. "It's all good, all good. Relieved to be able to talk about issues known only to myself."

For Lauren, it may very well have meant more.

CHAPTER TWENTY-SIX

Sitting at a table by the window facing the traffic going by, Dan breathed in deeply the aroma given off by his Starbucks dark roasted brew, which immediately recalled his own lawyer's coffee that day he discussed the case the prosecutor had made to the grand jury that week. This had all been brought back into focus by his conversation with Lauren the day before.

Mueller, his lawyer, had wasted no time in summing up where the legal issues facing his young client stood, staring directly across the mahogany table from Dan Marchetti in the Davis, Fromm, and Mueller law firm's conference room.

"Dan, you're being accused of expediting the deaths of Jane Salter and Joanne Cleary by altering their positive end-expiratory pressures to dangerous levels, resulting in cardiopulmonary arrests."

"Wait just a minute…"

"Dan, let me finish. Take notes, and I'll let you speak until your heart's content, afterward." Mueller had taken a sip from his coffee mug, which read, "World's Greatest Lawyer." Dan had prayed that that designation was true!

"Second, you're being charged with expediting the demise of a Roscoe Delmar. After diagnosing him with a dissecting abdominal aneurysm, you addressed his shock-like blood pressure with MAST trousers, amongst other treatments. The trousers were subsequently found to be deflated by an Emergency-Room nurse soon after the patient was pronounced dead from his ruptured aneurysm."

Dan had felt the heat in his neck surge as he was forced to listen to this crap.

"Third, your placement of a…" By now Mueller had dismissed any attempt to remember or correctly pronounce these medical terms, simply reading directly from his notes. "…Sengstaken-Blakemore tube directly led to the rupture of a patient's esophagus, again resulting in his death soon thereafter from overwhelming sepsis." Mueller had stopped for a moment to remove his eyeglasses and rub his tired, smallish, hazel-colored eyes. "Now, an erroneous interpretation by yourself of an electrocardiogram, whose machine was later found to be defective, possibly tampered with, will not be filed by the prosecution but may be slyly mentioned nevertheless…"

"Can I speak now?" Marchetti's face had registered total disgust. "What motive would I have to do these horrible things?"

"They claim you were obsessed with medical ethics, the 'status quo,' if you will, and endorsed euthanasia as a lawful and justifiable action."

"What? I categorically deny that. Where do they get that from?"

"They cite an incident in the ICU after the death of a Sarah Damen, when you vehemently criticized attendings and residents alike for, and I paraphrase, 'making a mockery of a human life.'"

"I did say that, but not for the reason you allude to. I had just lost a patient, who, I may add, died a heart-wrenching death, only to emerge from the room where a husband had thrown himself on the bed next to his beloved wife, to find the others discussing the pathophysiology of a 'saddle embolus' right outside the room. Heartless and inappropriate, for sure."

Mueller had busied himself taking notes, then continued, "There's also the matter of a debate as a student where you argued for the sanctity of euthanasia. Your word: 'sanctity'. What did you mean by that word? It's a little unusual."

Dan had sat back in his chair and just crumpled. "Oh my God, me? Were they all murdered and if so, why, in the name of God, would I do any such thing? What motive would…" He hadn't been able to finish the sentence, instead crashing his right arm down against the hard wood of the desk.

"All right, Dan," Mueller had said. "All right."

CHAPTER TWENTY-SEVEN

The 'General,' one of two urologists on staff, had earned his moniker due to his frequent reminders to anyone who would listen that he came from a proud military family in the Philippines. Back home, the only sign that his father felt anything at all for his only child would be an occasional pat on the head, and this only after pulling straight As on his report card, as any grade less was unacceptable and not worthy, whether he tried his best or not. His mother was terrified of his father, unable to defend herself at all when he berated her for burning dinner or spilling liquid on their floor, their pristine marble floor.

Following the surrender to the Japanese at Bataan and Corregidor, several groups of American and Filipino fighting men and women established guerrilla operations in the islands, his grandfather being one of them. For the remainder of the war, these guerrillas were supported and protected by the Filipino people. The guerrillas engaged in sabotage, fought the Japanese, and established a spy network, which eventually communicated Japanese military actions throughout the islands by radio to General MacArthur, then situated in Australia and ordered there by none other than FDR himself. The guerrilla network provided MacArthur with priceless information on Japanese troop deployments, location of aircraft, defense positions, and supply depots. The network also carefully identified the locations of Filipino and American POWs. No question existed whatsoever of their value to the Allied cause.

Needless to say, key values such as respect and acceptance were found throughout Filipino culture and even though the General had developed a thriving urologic practice since emigrating to the United States, he never felt as if his peers either respected nor accepted him into their fraternity.

To garner that respect, he slaved over building a financial empire. The General would engage in a practice he nicknamed "financial engineering," whereby he manufactured fake bills to send to Medicare for reimbursement. Since all insurance companies paid physicians less than they deserved, he rationalized, such engineering, though illegal, made him whole and the term itself made him see his actions as not possessing real-world consequences. Besides, he knew of several surgeons who engaged in similar practices and, believe it or not, he felt a certain need to conform. Then there was the matter of Dominic Antonetti, who had promised him millions of dollars in 'finder's fees' for providing the Medicare numbers of his entire patient inventory. Of course, they had their own model of financial engineering, though on steroids. Not to mention the advantageous financing given him for the opulent and expansive Surgi-Center he was constructing.

CHAPTER TWENTY-EIGHT

Carl Becker, MD would wince when reminded of growing up in Great Neck, Long Island, where three quarters of the student body were composed of fellow Jews from affluent families. His parents had moved from Brooklyn, Flatbush to be exact, where his mother Natalie had been surrounded by her four living siblings, each owning a home of their own on the block, 242 East 9th Street. Natalie's husband, Mordecai "Morty" Becker had worked his way up the Topp's baseball card business, finally leaving as this iconic family-run enterprise had earmarked the sons as future CEOs, leaving their invaluable employee with nowhere to continue to ascend. His move to Great Neck had represented a major step forward for his family, though he'd cautioned his two boys to note that their father earned nowhere near the income of the average homeowner in that wealthy area of Long Island.

"Become a professional, boys, or otherwise risk living like some schlepp somewhere you don't wish to be."

The boys, Carl and his older brother, Nathaniel, had been blessed with brains but were shortchanged physically. Stunted in stature throughout high school, no more than five foot four and with unusually short arms and ample noses, they had been unable to compete with the jocks and taller classmates. So, compensate they had, determined to become physicians who made a lot of money and dressed nicely. In fact, Carl had poured every dollar earned from odd jobs into clothes, preferring sport coats and expensive cuff-linked shirts to jeans or hoodies. The truth was, however, that such flashy displays of wealth, otherwise known as conspicuous consumption, led to increased selfishness. In fact, individuals like him developed jealousies of their high-minded colleagues who also achieved such a status. This in turn led to the same persons unfortunately being more likely to put their own needs ahead of doing the right thing. Such a man, or woman, aspires to a "winner-take-all" competition with others. They're more likely to cheat rather than face the consequences of losing. All this applied to Carl.

On this morning, Carl Becker stared at his spacious closet for what seemed like an eternity. He was now a short, rotund plastic surgeon with a decided paunch, a closely cropped beard dyed black, and a small thatch of hair (transplanted years before) that he maintained with meticulous care. This morning marked the first day of fall, so a suit with autumnal colors was in order lest someone notice an out-of-step fashion preference. This fascination with clothes began early as his father after leaving Topps had earned his living in the Manhattan garment center, opening a manufacturing plant specializing in female garments. Carl's brother, a cardiologist, one of Manhattan's finest, had his own affinity for expensive ties, no thrifty ticket item themselves since he discarded them after only wearing once.

Carl found himself unusually leveraged, with many Manhattan real estate holdings, plus homes in Provence, France, Palm Beach, Florida, and Park City, Utah.

To "make ends meet" the resourceful plastic surgeon added additional procedures that he'd never performed to a patient's bill. Such padding could easily account for $500,000 extra each year to his accounts receivable. In addition, a 'side' arrangement with Dominic Antonetti's people netted a hefty sum in exchange for insurance information to be sent in their direction.

Life was good.

***

Dominic Antonetti was about to place the book on a shelf in his library, having just finished it a few minutes earlier. After reading yet another biography of FDR (his obsession), this one written from the points of view of the four most trusted and longest serving members of his administration, Dominic decided to read again a particular passage pertaining to the longest-serving president. "He aroused devotion... Though he also had a heroic capacity to cause harm. He was ruthlessly self-centered, but his deviousness was the least attractive part of his disposition. Roosevelt surprisingly had a boundless interest in the shortcomings of those around him... But to succeed, he needed to mask his many resentments and cruelties."

Could this also be a description of himself? What motivates so-called good people to do bad things?

After all, hadn't Dominic given to an ample number of Italian charities? Did this compensate for his bad deeds?

Or was the tunnel vision he possessed to become the kind of success others could only envy in some ways obscuring his ability to show compassion?

Did the shitty way people treated him as a kid justify his actions now?

Was his envy of mafia bosses he knew due solely to his desire to belong?

There were so many difficult and uncomfortably probing questions.

CHAPTER TWENTY-NINE

Hamza Vipul had just seen his last patient that Wednesday afternoon. Thirty-five patients that day and still he barely made the living he craved. Born to the Qureshi caste but with a mother who was Finnish, Hamza knew that as far as Pakistanis were concerned, he was a mixed bag.

Qureshi signifies ancestry from the Quresh, the noblest Arab tribe that Prophet Muhammad belonged to. In South Asia, Qureshi is a multiethnic community spread across Pakistan, India, and Bangladesh. Most of the Qureshi reside in Sindh, since the Arabs settled down there and married local women. In the Indian state of Bihar, the Qureshi caste is primarily associated with the profession of butchery. The community members slaughter a wide variety of animals for halal meat, from goats to buffaloes.

Hamza would have none of this, as he would not take part in any traditional belief systems. Only forty, handsome, with an inordinately expensive wardrobe and a Corvette Stingray to drive, he remained a persistent source of aggravation to his father, Mohammed, a local business owner. "Mo," a mover and shaker in Hudson County, New Jersey, had begged Hamza to conform, but his having been born in the United States had forever severed any connection to Lahore.

Now his goals in life were quite simple. To make as much money as he possibly could from his medical profession, play the field, and get high as often as he could.

Unfortunately, Hamza, for some inexplicable reason at least to him, never received the type of recognition by his peers that he felt he'd earned. Quite the contrary—instead, a cloud of suspicion seemed to hover over his head. He'd been appointed the Program Director of the Internal Medicine Residency Program based on his superior clinical acumen and excellent instructing capabilities, but nevertheless, others felt he or his father had paid someone off in exchange for the much sought-after position. Not that such an arrangement was beyond him, for in his home country, such private quid-pro-quos were commonplace and not at all frowned upon. In fact, during the interview process for selecting the most academically gifted medical students to rank highly for his program, he let it be known that a fee of $25,000 would ensure their ranking on his list and would thus guarantee the computer match each medical student to his program, exceptional or not. Of course, it was entirely verboten to accept money, but since everyone suspected the worst when it came to explaining his successes, he felt he might as well comport himself in that manner. It was the so-called "Pygmalion effect." That is, if one is treated with suspicion, one's more likely to act in a way that justifies that perception.

Upon awakening, Hamza looked at himself in the bathroom mirror and liked what he saw. Dark jet-black hair that he routinely plied with gel, while taking great pains to trim his equally dark beard. His Armani suits were sharp looking and intended to impress a particular type of woman. His father, owner of a local Pakistani grocery store, also sat on the City Council and routinely hobnobbed with the Mayor, State Assemblymen, and even the Governor on occasion. This, of course, served to elevate his stature within the local Pakistani community and made his father stick out his chest with pride when addressed by others with deference. That too was Hamza's goal in life. To be addressed in such a fashion, to be held in such high esteem.

Working alongside Antonetti's associates certainly couldn't hurt.

CHAPTER THIRTY

Hank Van Patten was born into a real hardscrabble existence. His old man, in and out of prisons while he was young, was finally put away for good for running a lucrative car theft ring. The stolen vehicles would be given fraudulent vehicle identification numbers to be retitled and then resold online. In some cases, victims were allegedly confronted in their homes by members of the ring to steal their late-model vehicles. Finally, a large shipment was intercepted at Port Newark as more than five hundred stolen cars were being loaded into containers to be shipped overseas. Three strikes and he was gone forever.

The family went on food stamps. Hank's mother Rose worked as a hotel maid and at night in a laundromat cleaning up. Hank's sisters hooked up with riffraff to get out of the burdensome and somber household, then married hastily, gave birth, got divorced… No surprises there.

Hank shoplifted any chance he had and would volunteer as an altar boy, taking pains to observe the rules. For instance, he never crossed in front of the Holy Table but rather went behind it. Eventually, he reached the highest possible level, that of Guardian. The "compensation effect" was at work there, the tendency for people to assume that they accumulate moral capital by employing good deeds to balance out the bad ones. Or, as the school psychologist would later proclaim, Hank suffered from "cognitive dissonance," whereby people who do bad things ignore them because they can't tolerate the inconsistency between their behavior and their perceived selves.

In his spare time, Henry Van Patten loved to hang around Carl's Auto Body Shop, when he wasn't working at the hospital, the original owner having departed in a hurry when learning of a sting operation spearheaded by the FBI. Hank, still unmarried and unable to fill whatever free time he had with anything more enjoyable, loved to work with his hands. Sanding a damaged car's affected areas to remove any impurities on the surface, he would then either employ a suction machine or frame correction device depending on the dent depth. Afterwards, a coat of primer would be applied to the newly restored area, which allowed the fresh coat to stick and stay on the surface of the vehicle for a long time, even when exposed to harsh weather elements.

The hands-on aspect of the shop provided downtime to determine how best to scam the insurance companies, and customers alike, for that matter. Dishonesty in the repair shop extended beyond just charging the insurance company full cost. Charges for parts and other items delivered to the insurance company would be top dollar, while the vehicle owner would get replacement parts that were inferior, decrepit, or simply junk. Antonetti's people had been involved in 'chop shops' for many decades. Sending cars overseas had proved highly lucrative.

Why would a soon to be gastroenterologist do such a dishonorable thing?

Perhaps to demonstrate to his father his own bona fides in his line of work or simply to pay back his medical school loans faster.

CHAPTER THIRTY-ONE

"Lauren, we're all in agreement that we need to restart some heavy-duty meds to help clear up the problem in your lungs."

"You mean chemo, don't you, Dan? Quit with the euphemisms.'"

"Yes. I'll be more direct with you, I promise," he told her.

Before long, her chemo began to pace at a prescribed amount over time.

The anger she felt about carrying this burden of illness, especially at such a relatively young age, had taken hold. Maybe she was losing confidence in his skills as a physician, though he remained steadfast that he and the rheumatologist were on the absolute correct course. Though the circumstances couldn't be more disparate, Dan's mind couldn't help reverting to an extremely disconcerting time in his life.

"Nikki, can I ask you something?" Dan had clicked the remote and soon there was quiet. Nikki had been reading a magazine at the end of the sofa, and he felt a gaping separation, both physical and emotional. "Okay, I'm going to get right to the point. Since my arrest, I've felt you pull away from me, and I'm hurt beyond words. Do you think I'm guilty of those insane charges?"

Dan had stared accusingly at her almond-shaped eyes, which had lost the magical twinkle he'd been accustomed to admiring. Eyes were windows to the soul and hers had always managed to make him feel loved and, above all, safe. Eyes that registered full-throated acceptance and a growing pride for being attached at the hip to him.

"No, I don't think so, Dan." Nikki's denial hadn't matched her body language, though, which had looked defensive and closed. The truth was inextricably tied to all the trauma she'd sustained in her youth and her inherent distrust of everyone she encountered, which now included Dan. Except for the children in the pediatric ward. They were too young to develop those unflattering traits.

"You don't think so? What kind of fucked-up answer is that? You don't think so. You know what I think?" He'd paused to contain his surging anger and betrayal. "I think..." Dan hadn't been able to finish, overwhelmed with a sense of indescribable loneliness and of being on a tiny island with no friends, no career, and no future.

The brokenhearted intern had grabbed his Pirates windbreaker. "Going to wander a bit. Right now, I can't imagine how you'd even consider me capable of murder, Nikki."

She'd watched him leave, her mouth agape, though, the man she'd been convinced could do no wrong was probably nothing more than a fantasy now. Doubts were worsening every day, rather than lessening as she'd hoped. Her migraines the past few days had reared their ugly heads, a phenomenon that always followed when her mind was deeply troubled.

CHAPTER THIRTY-TWO

It happened innocently enough. A typical Sunday night for Marchetti.

"Dr. Marchetti, it's Alfonso; sorry to bother you, sir." Alfonso was one of Dan's best residents and the most dependable. Marchetti trusted him more than other residents to be his eyes and ears if he couldn't be on site when on call. "Sir, we've had a bona fide Goodpasture's Syndrome admitted tonight to your service. He came with a stack of papers detailing his entire history. He's a thirty-year-old Air Force pilot. Biopsy proven, positive anti-glomerular basement membrane antibody, Ommaya reservoir in his left supraclavicular region, urine loaded with red blood cells."

Dan loved this guy: no nonsense and to the point. The staccato delivery gave him all the pertinent facts. This patient had a proven rare disease that had required an indwelling catheter to help with medication delivery.

"How's he doing clinically?" Dan asked.

"Severe pain, otherwise stable."

Renal colic given blood in the urine and pain? Dan had never taken care of a patient with this condition before, but he knew these patients did bleed in their kidneys and sometimes lungs. An internist, even one involved in a teaching program all his professional life, may see only one case in a career. To date, he'd seen two.

"He's getting a morphine IV to make him comfortable," Alfonso continued.

Dan responded, "Make sure you start high-dose steroids. Have rheumatology see him, and we need to alert the plasmapheresis team to cleanse his blood of the abnormal proteins." He paused to think of other issues and hit upon the kidneys and lungs. "What are his creatinine and pulse oximetry?"

"Both good at 1.2 and 98 percent on room air," Alfonso responded. He'd anticipated all questions appropriately.

"Call me if anything changes. I'll see him in the morning, unless of course you need me to come in now."

"Not necessary, sir."

Little did he realize how wrong he had been.

***

The self-professed Navy pilot looked at the intern and spoke clearly and succinctly.

"I have Goodpasture's Syndrome and am in a great deal of pain. These are my records."

With that, the handsome and fit-looking African American man of thirty years held out the thick folder containing his complete medical records to his assigned first-year resident, Arthur Leavitt.

"Thank you." The young physician began reading through the files when his patient interrupted.

"I'm slated to receive the Medal of Freedom from the President for my past military service, but unfortunately I'll obviously be unable to attend the ceremony in two days."

This little aside was not in the script, an ad-lib.

"Really?" Returning to the file, Arthur observed, "I see you've had three renal biopsies, have an indwelling Omaya Reservoir for IV meds and have been on every immunosuppressive therapy in the books, including plasmapheresis."

"That's true. Listen, I'm in a great deal of discomfort from the kidney bleeding. Morphine's the only medicine that helps with this problem."

"I'd look to take some of your urine down to the lab, centrifuge it, and then look under the microscope. We can give you some painkillers after I finish my exam."

Within the next thirty minutes, Dan had done just what he told him he would do, with five medical students in tow.

"What do you guys expect to see under the microscope?" He inquired of his student doctors. One by one they took turns examining the urinary sediment on the slide. This was the gravelly material that was left in the bottom of the tube after spending five minutes in the centrifuge, a piece of equipment that spun up to 15,000 revolutions per minute, depending on its size and components.

"Lots of red blood cells," the more intrepid ones offered in unison.

"Exactly. Now, do they look normal or dysmorphic?"

No response.

"Okay, you'll need to look at a lot of normals before being able to determine the abnormals. The answer is that they're completely normal and, furthermore, there are no casts. Not what we'd expect to see with Goodpasture's Syndrome. I'm baffled right now."

CHAPTER THIRTY-THREE

"My name is Dr. Dante Marchetti, an internist here in New Jersey, and I'm calling you regarding one of your former Navy pilots, who's a patient of mine. Essentially, I need confirmation that the medical records he handed us belong to him."

"I take it you don't believe him?" The Navy clerk responded.

"Let's just say his case raises more questions than answers."

"I see. Please fax us his information and we'll check. Our fax is…"

Dan complied after hanging up the phone.

"Dr. Marchetti, your patient just spiked a temp to 105 degrees but looks great. You know, not for nothing, but there's something strange about that guy."

"105? Not toxic-looking?" Dan shook his head, then, "Strange, you say?"

"Not at all ill-appearing, too smooth, too practiced, if you get my drift?"

Never ignore the observations of an experienced nurse, and if you do, do so at your own peril.

Once inside the room, his patient informed Dan, "You may be getting a call from my sister, who's a pulmonary doctor in Seattle, sometime today."

"Really?" Dan responded. "You've been here four days already and she hasn't called yet, her brother who has Goodpasture's Syndrome?"

"She's busy. Dr. Marchetti, I believe the cause of my disease was my exposure to jet fuel in the Navy."

"There's little data supporting that and not at all definitive. You seem to know a good deal about your illness."

"Got to if I want to stay alive."

"You know, we called the home number listed on your form and a man answered. He became irate. Said you've never lived there and to stop giving out that number."

"I just moved and don't have a phone."

"I heard you convinced one of my interns to pay for your phone here so the President could congratulate you on being awarded the Congressional Medal of Honor. Did he call?"

"Yes, he did."

How come when I Googled you, I came up with nothing? A Congressional Medal of Honor winner?

"Okay, now, we treated you with strong medicines and are considering plasmapheresis. Still in a lot of pain?"

The patient nodded.

"Getting a lot of morphine, I see."

"Not enough."

This fish is starting to stink to high heaven.

CHAPTER THIRTY-FOUR

Dan sipped his scotch as he sat in his favorite reading chair, that week's *New England Journal of Medicine* having just arrived, every Thursday like clockwork. Staring at the front cover, he perused the articles and saw one entitled "The Red Baron," which piqued his interest. It was a case report—he always found these fascinating— of a so-called "zebra," an unusual case, of the kind that Mass General always seemed to receive through its world-famous doors. His eyes widened.

Thirty-year-old Navy pilot admitted with Goodpasture's Syndrome...

"I don't fuckin' believe it, this is about my guy." Dan rifled through the pages to get to it, the lengthy story taking at least fifteen minutes to digest. The Red Baron described his patient having stolen paperwork from a Navy seaman who had Goodpasture's Syndrome. This impostor had been hospitalized in thirteen different facilities on the East Coast, from Florida all the way to New Jersey. He'd received numerous toxic medications, underwent three renal biopsies, and had numerous microscopic analyses of his urine, to which three nephrologists retrofitted their findings to fit his fake diagnosis. The motive seemed to be to secure powerful opiates. Why else?

Of course, the lawsuits hadn't been filed yet.

"Unbelievable," he muttered out loud. He reached for the phone and dialed the floor.

"Five West."

"Good evening. It's Dr. Marchetti. Can you get me the charge nurse, please?"

"Speaking, Dr. Marchetti. We're a little short-staffed, so I'm answering the phones also—Mary Smith here."

"Hi, Mary. Listen, our Navy pilot is a phony and…"

"Doc, we know. The resident read the article too and confronted him with it. He's threatening to bolt, but of course, he's too comfortable here to do so. We see all kinds, huh?"

We will not have heard the last from this debacle. Not at all.

***

"My friend, it's time for you to gather your personal items and plan on leaving my hospital soon." Dan stared at his clever patient with the elaborate story that was all based on lies.

The faux Navy pilot held out his hands as if to say, "What the fuck are you talking about?"

"Oh please… We know you stole those medical records from someone else in the Navy who really suffered from Goodpasture's Syndrome, wove a very imaginative but made-up tale concerning yourself, and essentially put yourself in harm's way. In fact, we'll send you home on meds for the tuberculosis that came about because we were forced to treat your made-up disease with powerful drugs. They ultimately suppressed your immune system, thus allowing the TB organism to grow. That's all on you, my friend. What I can't figure out is the 'why.' Of course, this fits nicely in the 'Munchausen' diagnostic category, which probably explains everything."

"Kicking out a sick patient's fine with me, Doc, but you'll be hearing from my lawyer shortly," the patient threatened with a knowing smile.

"Really? I'm nosy—on what grounds?"

Crickets.

***

"Dr. Marchetti? Agent Forsythe of the Federal Bureau of Investigation."

Dan had just finished his work for the day and was about to leave when he received this unexpected visitor.

"Oh, the FBI, how… How can I help you?" Dan inquired haltingly. Events from years back were destined to never leave the deep recesses of his mind, he reasoned repeatedly.

"A patient whose care you've been involved with is part of a vast conspiracy to defraud physicians and hospitals nationwide by establishing malpractice suits based on Munchausen cases erroneously treated, and to seek severe punitive damages for negligence. Your patient—"

Dan interrupted the agent mid-sentence. "I know who it is." He shook his head in disgust.

"There's more. We have reason to believe organized crime brutally muscled the brains behind the operation to curry favor with healthcare institutions they wish to do business with and thus eliminate the lawsuits. We are presently investigating one organization in your area who appear to maintain serious links with the Russian mafia in Brooklyn."

"I see. Will keep this information in mind."

"Good. Dr. Marchetti, we'll be in touch if we need to speak with you further."

CHAPTER THIRTY-FIVE

Dan ambled over to the front door when he heard his sickly chime go off.

Got to get that guy fixed already, must be the wiring.

"Certified letter, need your signature, sir."

"Okay. What the…?" The letter was from a well-known malpractice law firm in the area. "I'm getting sued?" He asked rhetorically. What else could it be?

Quickly dispatching with the envelope, he perused the letter as he oftentimes did for key phrases. "Miller and Dornfeld has been retained… To resolve a medical negligence claim without protracted litigation whereby…"

Dan felt all the air exit his lungs while a pain seared through his gut.

A Munchausen patient was suing him for failing to recognize immediately that he was pretending to be sick all along, even though the medical records he stole and passed off as his own were fake! Un-fucking-believable!

The fact was that in this instance, an individual with excellent clinical sense concocted a story, replete with fake labs, biopsy, and scans, that if a clinician didn't take seriously after the patient presented with signs and symptoms of a dangerous disease, the outcome could be fatal. Furthermore, extracting blood from an indwelling catheter to squirt into a urine sample to document blood in the urine and managing to play havoc with the thermometer to register a high fever would never be suspected normally. Who does this? If this case wasn't thrown immediately out of court, then what faith could one have in the legal system going forward?

Déjà vu all over again.

***

"Please take a seat, Dr. Marchetti."

Dan looked around at the conference table in the boardroom and noticed a number of nattily dressed men, one in his fifties, another late sixties or so, and one man and one woman in their late thirties, he surmised. All were lawyers except for the woman, who was introduced as a spokesperson for the hospital's medical malpractice insurer.

"Dr. Marchetti, I'm Richard Brennan, one of the outside counsels for the hospital. We're here to discuss a few items, one being this malpractice suit that was filed on behalf of an individual, a Brian Casey, alleging gross negligence involving his medical care." He proceeded to name the dates and issues with his care rendered during that time by Marchetti.

"You're familiar with the case?" He asked rhetorically.

"Yes, yes, I am," Dan responded firmly with the slightest tinge of defensiveness.

This whole scene is too fuckin' familiar, though the circumstances are completely different this time around.

"Please instruct us all what you know about the case."

Dan proceeded to recount the case step by step as it unfolded, only occasionally looking down at his notes to confirm dates and exact lab data.

"The patient, or someone else, had stolen the medical records from a Navy pilot who he knew suffered from the heretofore mentioned 'Goodpasture's Syndrome.'"

One of the younger lawyers interjected, "Are you aware that this particular patient had been hospitalized at least half a dozen times in the tri-state area and had undergone renal biopsies, had inserted indwelling catheters, and received powerful immunosuppressive medications, the latter from yourself as well?"

"I've since learned as much, in fact it was over a dozen on the East Coast but had no knowledge of this beforehand. Obviously."

"How is that possible in this age of electronic medical records and the like?"

"Simple. These separate EMRs do not yet talk with each other unless they are part of the same healthcare system. I imagine the people behind these cases knew that beforehand."

"Okay. Okay. But are you aware that each hospital has settled their cases out of court for rather massive sums?"

"No, I'm not aware of this. But if this is true—and I have no reason to doubt your word—such action in my opinion represents a travesty of justice, plain and simple."

"It would appear so. But Dr. Marchetti, the tuberculosis that the patient contracted, he alleges, because of your care, has wreaked havoc within his body and now resides in his bone marrow, brain, and of course lungs. Furthermore, Dr. Marchetti, it's resistant to anti-tuberculous medication, so-called multi-resistant TB."

"Yes, I'm aware, all due undoubtedly to this elaborate farce he undertook, which necessitated immune-suppressive drugs, therefore leading to TB. Mr. Casey has only himself to blame. Let me be crystal clear. If he'd had the disease and we hadn't treated empirically, he most assuredly would have succumbed. Let me go further. If you were his doctor, what would you have done?"

Now, that did sound defensive.

"I can't answer that, but he didn't have the disease, Doctor." He paused a second before following with this comment. "As this case pertains to you and the hospital, who insures you, and owing to your full-time employed physician status, they're seeking sums that far exceed any reasonable settlement. One hundred million dollars in damages."

Dan sat motionless at the news. The figure was outrageous, of course. What was there left to say?

"Though important, this issue is not the only issue we wish to discuss today, Doctor," another voice chimed in.

Dan twisted his head ever so slightly at this last comment.

A member of the Board, Alex Brightman, a successful self-made businessman who prospered in the exploding real-estate market after being given a significant head start from his father, continued. "No, we're here today to discuss your taking over the reins of Sacred Heart Hospital. That is, to become our next Chief Executive Officer and President." With that, the room erupted with applause.

How strange. Obviously, they view the malpractice suit just as I do.

Dan repositioned himself awkwardly in his chair.

Don't appear surprised even though you're gobsmacked by this offer.

"CEO—that's quite a step up for me. After our previous CEO was dismissed, I assumed the position would go to the interim person, our CFO, Mark Schwartz, until a national search could be undertaken?"

"To be perfectly honest, both paths were considered, but owing to the real leadership vacuum and tremendous distrust voiced on the part of the medical staff in our Administration, we believe hiring a well-respected and admired physician would be a logical next choice." Brightman smiled, his perfectly capped teeth and obvious hair transplant not at all natural-looking or pleasing to the eye.

"I see. That's flattering. Can I think about it?"

Don't appear too eager but what a career milestone for a man who hasn't yet reached fifty!

"Of course, of course. Very understandable. One thing—you'd clearly have to curtail your clinical time significantly, but certainly not altogether. The medical staff would relate well to a CEO still in touch with patients, credibility, you know."

Dan nodded. "I understand. I'll be in touch shortly with my decision. I must say that I'm leaning towards taking it."

The next day he gladly accepted. This would represent a real opportunity to make a difference… Perhaps.

CHAPTER THIRTY-SIX

Dan sat around all weekend contemplating being the CEO in the only hospital he'd ever worked in, dating back to externships as a medical student, residency training in Internal Medicine and now attending physician. Obviously, the powers that be believed he possessed the qualities to do the job well and the integrity to do the right thing in difficult circumstances. Or so he believed, though the more he thought about it, the more doubts crept in. But Dan was as stubborn a man as there was when it came to following the dictates of his convictions.

An incident in medical school came to mind where standing up against a bullying attending physician brought him nothing but grief in the short run. Those were the days when medical students were expected to be seen and not heard. Dante, having learned too late of a fistfight that broke out between this guy and one of the best students in his class the previous month, had naively signed up for the nephrology elective with the asshole. Why hadn't he done some research on this instructor beforehand? There had been forty-nine other possible selections.

The incident began when Dr. Lowenstein had declared right out of the box, "I hope you're not an idiot like the previous medical student."

Twenty minutes later, when it came time to present the patient he had just examined, Lowenstein had pumped him repeatedly with questions in a staccato manner, Dan successfully answering each one.

"Go see another patient now," he'd ordered, his face registering disappointment, it seemed to Dan. Turning to do so, Lowenstein threw out another question. "What's the mechanism for Alpha Methyl Dopa?" Dan hesitated, caught off guard, and responded incorrectly. "Wrong answer, my friend. Pretty basic stuff. You're going to have a hard time getting through school, never mind becoming anything more than a mediocre physician."

"How is that, because I gave a wrong answer?"

"Go see another patient," Lowenstein had remarked with a dismissive wave of his hand, ignoring Dan's retort. Dan had dutifully made his way to a patient's room when he suddenly stopped, reversing his field.

"Let me ask you something, Dr. Lowenstein. Do you truly believe your method of instructing works, however harsh, or do you ask questions solely for the express desire to demean, to make one feel small? Because if it's the latter, then that's not acceptable behavior anywhere!"

Holy shit. Speaking back to a medical school professor can only lead to bad things. And it had. The asshole had reported him to the Dean of Students, who'd reprimanded him in his office in what could only be described as a kangaroo court. The problem was simple. Dan's mother had taught the boys to stand up for themselves when they were being wronged by someone, otherwise they'd lose respect for themselves.

Fast-forward twenty years. It almost played out like an O'Henry story when Dan was about to hire a geriatrician for his faculty practice. The candidate had proven to be an excellent fit and, providing the references panned out, the job was his.

"Everything looks in order. Let me call your references…" After Dr. Srinivasan exited his office, Dan picked up the phone to call the first name on the list, anxious to conclude this hiring process. The name was Dr. Lowenstein, geriatrician in Boca Raton, Florida. Couldn't be the same guy. That guy was a nephrologist in the northeast. Besides, Lowenstein was a common Jewish surname.

"Hello, I'd like to speak with Dr. Lowenstein, whose name was given to me as a reference for a Dr. Srinivasan. I'm Dr. Dante Marchetti."

"Oh sure, one minute. Dr. Srinivisan's been a joy," the assistant offered gladly.

Before long, Dr. Lowenstein's voice began jovially, "I know you."

Dan froze. They were one and the same. But he didn't miss a beat.

"And I know you. In fact, I point to your horrible behavior twenty years ago as an example to my children as to how not to treat another human being."

"Well," Lowenstein cleared his throat, taken aback by the unexpectedly brazen response. "Let me take this moment to apologize to you from the bottom of my heart. You see, I wasn't a very nice person back then."

Did I hear this correctly? The man's demonstrating true contrition.

"Of course, I accept your apology. It takes a real person of character to offer that after all these years."

"Thank you, Dan. By the way, Dr. Srinivasan will make an excellent addition to your staff." A stroke had nearly killed the man and afterwards, he had an epiphany, according to the newly hired geriatrician when told of the conversation.

This was how Dan rolled.

CHAPTER THIRTY-SEVEN

"You seem preoccupied, Dan. What's on your mind?" Lauren, now feeling much better with the new drug regimen, sat up in her hospital bed. Looking out the window, she felt buoyed by the skies, a cerulean blue, cloudless, and seemingly magical.

"Well, I got a notice today that I'm being sued for care I rendered to a patient with Munchausen Syndrome. I don't suppose you've heard of this strange malady?"

"Well, I know about Munchausen by proxy, so it must be that the patient himself or herself pretends to have a disease instead of causing their child to become sick."

"Right you are. Well, this guy gets admitted to me who has stolen someone else's medical records, pretends to be that patient, and in fact manages to simulate several signs and symptoms to make it look believable. Soon after his initial admission we uncovered the ruse, but before we could do so, we had to empirically treat or otherwise potentially lose the patient."

"By empirically, you mean before you had hard evidence, for then it could be too late? Why do people do this kind of thing?"

"Traumatic childhood? Either abuse from family members, loss of a loved one at a young age, or abandonment, I'm told."

Just the repercussions I tried to head off when the twins became orphaned years back.

In truth, weeks after Dan had been exonerated from any wrongdoing over the deaths at Deerwood Hospital, he'd tried to speak with the twins' aunt, who'd been awarded temporary custody pending the verdict. But placing a call to the home phone only revealed a discontinued service announcement. Something inside him had made him uneasy, as if she'd perhaps escaped to somewhere with them as she'd threatened to do so in the past. Arriving at the condominium, his heartbeat had quickened as he'd noticed the drapes had been removed, while his peering through the windows revealed the rooms devoid of furniture. For all intents and purposes, there had been no trace of any inhabitants, at least the ones he was looking for. Could it be that Geri Marchand, their impulsive and somewhat erratic aunt, had taken the children and disappeared, probably having heard of his acquittal? Perhaps she'd believed the charges and saw his being freed as a result of a clever lawyer's maneuvering. Dan had leaned against the car and cried unabashedly, haunted by vivid memories of the little girl with a 104-degree temperature who he'd soaked in a tub of lukewarm water to bring the high fever down. Or of the boy pulling a lounge chair and accidentally falling in the deep water of the town pool, Dan jumping in fully clothed to save him before he could swallow any appreciable amount of water.

"I will never give up trying to find them," he'd promised himself.
***

"What can I do for you, Mr. Antonetti?" Dan inquired, his first full day as CEO starting off with a purposeful meeting.

"Well, first, thank you for making the time to see me. I know you're a busy man."

"Not a problem. One of our Board members, Bruce Kaplan, relayed to me your interest in meeting. Classmate of yours in grade school, I believe."

They both chuckled, a Cheshire grin appearing on the mobster's ruggedly masculine face.

"Bruce and I go way back, and he's a very successful lawyer, I understand. Let me get right to the point if I may."

"Certainly."

"My businesses involve such sizeable and diverse industries as funeral parlors and unions representing a number of hospital employee groups, amongst many others." Antonetti handed a list of healthcare-related businesses to Marchetti, who took a moment to study the list before once again making eye contact.

"Very impressive."

"I've taken the liberty to spell out the numerous ways we can help the hospital improve its bottom line significantly, beginning with some of the litigation you are facing presently."

"Oh?"

Forsythe's forewarning had been a timely one.

"Your own case involving the Munchausen patient. A similar one, I might add, played itself out at a hospital in Los Angeles, resulting in a jury awarding the patient $100 million dollars back in the fall."

"Our lawyers have informed me of that judgement, but I can't really discuss…"

Antonetti held up his right hand. "Say no more. It's just that the group behind these actions are no longer willing to settle these cases for what they consider a pittance when they can land such hefty awards as this. That hospital became insolvent."

"Yes, I'm aware. How could you help?" Dan probed his visitor further.

"We already have."

"How's that?" The CEO leaned forward in his chair, interested.

"Let's just say that their star witness against you had a change of heart."

"A change of heart? How so?"

"Consider this a 'good faith' gesture. We need to keep our hospitals and healthcare institutions in good financial standing if our communities are to flourish." With that the peripatetic "businessman" stood up to leave, but not before leaving his business card on top of his pro forma. "Let's stay in touch."

These men besmirched the proud Italian heritage in a way that Dan and his family always found abhorrent, with values that contradicted their family's of hard, honest work and a charitable heart. Up until now, Dan had never had any dealings with the like.

CHAPTER THIRTY-EIGHT

Dominic Antonetti exited the shower quickly, as he was running late for an appointment that morning. He'd managed to oversleep, as he'd been out late the night before playing cards and drinking at the Club Savory. Today he and the rest of the hospital board needed to meet with Dr. Marchetti, the new Sacred Heart Hospital CEO and discuss the fiscal health, as it were, of their beloved institution. The board members spoke glowingly of his energy and his purported clinical acumen, felt to be superlative. Marchetti's peers described him as "a doctor's doctor," a high compliment. Antonetti suspected that Marchetti must have known that they essentially made quite a leap of faith to choose someone without any significant administrative experience for such a prestigious position.

That's precisely where the feeling of indebtedness should factor in.

Within the hour, the Board Chairman deposited himself in front of the CEO, his hangover headache now a thing of the past thanks to a few Motrin.

"Doctor, so nice to see you again so soon. I trust you've settled in nicely and hit the ground running," he said, taking that moment to pop open his briefcase and retrieve a manila folder with some papers inside. Placing it on the boardroom table, he pushed the folder forward towards Dan, indicating that he wanted him to scan the information contained within.

Dan obliged dutifully, as even this neophyte knew that developing an amicable and solid relationship with the hospital's Chairman of the Board

Antonetti and other members represented an integral first step in ensuring his support.

"The board has taken the time before you came aboard to highlight steps needed to help restore some fiscal stability to Sacred Heart in this time of drastically reduced reimbursements, unfunded mandates for healthcare institutions, and the devastating financial debacle of the Covid pandemic."

"You're referring to the twenty-million-dollar shortfall this year to date."

"Yes, yes I am." His friendly smile was now replaced with an ominous frown and deep sigh.

Glancing at the top sheet, Dan noted the prominent mention of Bellecon Associates, a healthcare entity with which he had no familiarity.

"Who are Bellecon Associates?"

"Healthcare consultants who'll help us right-size and get our financial house in order, especially as pertaining to new revenue streams."

"I see. But as the Chief Executive Officer, I'll have final say in who we bring onboard, will I not?"

"Of course, of course. But surely you can understand our reluctance to wait until you come up to speed to right our ship, which, I may remind you, has been listing badly."

"I see," Dan responded weakly, surprised at his own timidity in the face of such hubris.

Something already doesn't sound right. What dangerous waters am I swimming in? Am I just here to rubber-stamp their decisions, and is this a Board decision or Antonetti's himself? After all, his hard-driving, abrasive personality, and ruthlessness when it came to business dealings are well known.

CHAPTER THIRTY-NINE

"What do you think of our new CEO?" The "General" inquired of the physicians seated at his table in the Doctors' Lounge at Sacred Heart Hospital.

Hamza, Hank, and Carl had just arrived at the newly refurbished physician-only dining area, now hosting a series of hot meals laid out on a buffet-style table with generous amounts prepared by the cafeteria people each day.

Nothing was too good for the people who bring the patients to the hospital.

"He just has the look of someone who isn't destined to last any longer than the others," Carl offered, stuffing a hefty piece of meatloaf into his mouth.

"Seriously," the General persisted, "what effect's he going to have on my bottom line?"

"How do you mean?" Hamza inquired.

"For one, interfering with the status quo, as it were," Carl answered without being asked directly. "I think what the General's getting at is clamping down on some of our more imaginative methods of keeping ourselves whole."

The others nodded accordingly, no more needing to be said out loud. With insurance companies squeezing them to death and overheads climbing, interference with the status quo would be the last thing they needed.

***

"Nice putt, Dan," Drew Higgins, the architect for the new hospital, said as the two of them sauntered off their first green. This was the hospital's yearly golf outing and an enormous fundraising event.

"So, you designed the hospital?" The newly appointed CEO inquired as they both took their seats in the golf cart, soon on their way to the scenic but very short par three-hole, Lady Liberty standing majestically on their right there at the famous Liberty National.

"It was my architectural firm that designed the building, but getting the Board of Directors to agree to where they wanted it to stand on the acreage posed a real issue, in fact, a year-long debate."

"Why was that?"

Higgins, a lean but very lanky gentleman with short white hair neatly combed to the side, and a ruddy complexion most likely worsened by a pop or two at breakfast, turned to face his golf partner. This fundraising outing was a highpoint each summer for most of the entrants.

"Simple, half the board was nervous about the possibility of digging up mob-related bodies during the excavation."

Dan stared at the affable but street-savvy architect. "Drew, you can't be serious!"

"As God is my witness. One word of caution, Dan, and you didn't hear this from me. There are several 'connected' individuals on the Board of Directors, so tread very carefully in those waters now that you're a big honcho."

"Thank you for the advice. Including the Chairman of the Board?"

"Especially the Chairman."

Certainly, has been an interesting day so far.

CHAPTER FORTY

"Rich, can you wheel me over to my sister's room so I can visit with her?" Scott asked his male nurse after learning that both were hospitalized at the same time. Lauren's disease activity had ramped up yet again.

"Let me finish a few things and then, no problem, bud." Nursing was a second career for this former IT person, who'd found the tech world extremely unfulfilling, especially following the Covid 19 pandemic. Simply put, he needed people contact to feel less lonely and isolated, so nursing fit the bill.

Ten minutes later, true to his word, the balding, stockily built forty-two-year-old nurse pushed his patient into the elevator and down two floors to the ICU. Before long, Scott found himself across from his sister, who'd just been placed in a spacious comfort chair for her obligatory "out of bed" time that morning.

They fervently gripped each other's hands, their embrace speaking volumes.

"How're you feeling, sis?"

"Hey, Scott. Must be all these meds but been dreamin' about when we were told about our mother having died. I kept envisioning Mom and I recall repeating that I couldn't sleep without our mother. Strange. I've never found peace since." Lauren shook her head and was interrupted by a violent cough.

Scott blurted out, "For myself, I used silence as a coping strategy, bottling up my feelings when it came to talking about her death."

They hugged spontaneously, a rare event in these tumultuous days.

"I could only depend on you, Lauren, and of course, myself."

"I know. I know, my sweet brother."

CHAPTER FORTY-ONE

Today marked four weeks exactly since Marchetti had taken over the role of Chief Executive Officer and President of Sacred Heart Hospital. Getting tutorials on the fine points of budgeting, business plan development, fundraising, and so forth seemed direct and not particularly difficult for the newly appointed administrator, though he had to drastically curtail his clinical time for the ever-increasing number of duties and responsibilities in this vaunted role.

That was why he decided to periodically slip into the morning report that the Internal Medicine Residency Program held every day to hear cases admitted to the Teaching Service. Remaining clinically sharp was so important to him. Today, however, Marchetti heard presented two cases horribly mismanaged by the attendings of the patients, and unfortunately, the residents involved learned the hard way about the dreaded consequences of poor clinical decision-making.

After a moment, he gathered himself enough to speak in a controlled but pointed manner.

"Let me get this straight. A seventeen-year old full-term pregnant woman received an epidural before delivering, complained of a constant headache after going home, came back to the Emergency Room for treatment, was given pain medication, sent home again, and ultimately died when she lost so much cerebrospinal fluid that the traction exerted on the blood vessels in her brain led to bilateral subdural hematomas and eventual brain herniation and death."

The resident presenting shook his beleaguered head in agreement.

"And furthermore, this was the second patient in two months that died in the same hellacious way?" His eyes snapped shut, his fists banging the sides of his chair. "Let me guess. Another minority woman."

"Yes."

"Of course. And both were assumed to be drug-seeking and given little credence to their stories. What the hell were the anesthesiologists using for needles, trocars? And the ER docs, didn't they learn anything after the first death?" Marchetti gathered himself. "Now listen," he began slowly, "not knowing about this potential complication I suppose in some circles could constitute a reasonable explanation for negligent acts. Point of fact, I, along with an attending, failed to diagnose a case of 'necrotizing fasciitis' in a diabetic man when I was a resident many years ago. Had never seen it, relied on my attending's superior knowledge base, and treated appropriately for cellulitis in a diabetic. Though we started the appropriate antibiotics and asked for an infectious disease consult, the absolutely correct next step would've been sending the patient immediately to the operating room for extensive debridement. The man succumbed to his infection the next day. But—and a big but here involves this second pregnant woman. This was the second time in one month this rare complication had occurred. Ladies and gentlemen, totally inexcusable!"

Dan left the room more crestfallen than incensed. Such was the value he put on human life.

The incidence of one of these tragedies was infinitesimally small, but two in two months is as rare as they come, Goddammit.

CHAPTER FORTY-TWO

"Russell Cronenworth? I'm Dr. Dan Marchetti, the CEO of this hospital. I understand you requested to see me." Dan reached over to put his hand on the patient's shoulder, who he'd just learned had become a quadriplegic following emergency neurosurgery required following a serious car accident. Sustaining an unstable cervical neck fracture, Dr. Richard Robinson, a new neurosurgeon added to the Zampuso practice, had been called to operate and prevent loss of motor function. Though the patient was able to move all four extremities initially, the post-op findings were anything but positive.

"Sir, that surgeon came to my bedside to inform me that he was going to stabilize my neck but reeked of alcohol on his breath." Russell's voice raised indignantly, but returned to speaking softly, unable to summon the continuous strength to express his true outrage. He still felt the effects of the anesthesia and soreness from the previous endotracheal tube placement.

"Did Dr. Robinson appear inebriated, Russell?" Dan inquired, anxious to determine his surgeon's state of sobriety.

"Inebriated, sir?"

"Drunk?"

"I believe he was, as he slurred his speech and his eyes looked red and glassy."

Dan stiffened. It was not the first time he'd heard such a complaint about a physician on duty, though this time, the result appeared to be catastrophic, and he was in a position to do something about it. Marchetti needed to put a stop to this, even if it meant reducing the number of neurosurgeons available in the county when specialists in this area had reached a critically low number.

***

"My Dante, a CEO of a hospital! *Che bello, che bello!*" Dan's mother screamed during the family celebration at the Mamma Mia restaurant, his father having reserved the back room for twenty family members and friends.

"*Magari!*" The room erupted when Uncle Sal suggested that the Presidency of the United States was next. The wine had been flowing, but indeed they were all so proud, especially aware of all that he'd been through in his five decades of life.

"Now to find a sweet Italian girl to share your life with is what your blessed father and I always wished for you, *caro!*"

On the surface Dan smiled broadly and often, but deep down, he felt an unsettling feeling, as if the pasta with tomato sauce was about to repeat on him. It was a new chapter indeed with his promotion, or would it be a trip through Dante's Inferno again? The truth was that Dante Marchetti didn't trust the staying power of good fortune.

CHAPTER FORTY-THREE

How would members of the medical staff react to one of their own receiving the nod for such a prestigious position? Again, his mind reflected on a teaching position he'd accepted years before when the CEO chose to issue him a raise after six months in his role there.

The cold shoulder Dan had receiving from the other physicians at his first academic position began suddenly afterwards, when no one sought him out for lunch, hallway chats, or even collegial case discussions.

Finishing rounds one Saturday morning, Dan had passed one of his colleagues, Dr. Paula Grange, who'd ignored his greeting and continued walking.

"Excuse me, Paula, but have I offended you somehow?"

"Yes, you did."

"Can you please enlighten me so I can make amends?" Dan had asked disbelievingly.

"Simple, you received a huge raise and the prestige that goes with that position. Who wouldn't be upset? That's human nature, my friend."

***

Dominic gazed out at the calm, blue-green water that Aruba was known for along with the gentle trade winds that made it one of his favorite places to vacation with his family and, frankly, unwind. He'd purchased a home there a few years back, whose value had skyrocketed due to the government severely capping all building, an effort to prevent overrunning the island's beauty and desirability.

"Dad, come with us!" Shouted his teenage daughters, having signed up for parasailing. Dominic demurred, his fear of heights keeping him grounded. Besides, that was a young person's indulgence. Now that he'd developed several superbly profitable enterprises, he needed time to contemplate some of his next moves upon returning to New Jersey. Certain individuals had to be "straightened out," like that hospital CEO Marchetti who'd yet to get the message apparently that he needed to come aboard or risk repercussions.

Sure, he was obstinate, but Dominic felt strongly that he'd eventually come around.

CHAPTER FORTY-FOUR

Marchetti exited the parking lot just in time to observe Dr. Hamza Vipul drive through in his bright red Lamborghini, a car that cost a laughable amount of money, at least 300K. Where does an internist get that kind of money? Even though he was rewarded for his excellent teaching with the Program Director position of the Internal Medicine Residency Program, the additional stipend would still make affording such a car highly implausible. Furthermore, Dan knew his father was a State Assemblyman from their county who also owned a small Pakistani restaurant in town. So, family money seemed unlikely. No, when he'd been informed by a disgruntled intern of Pakistani heritage that he was forced to pay $25,000 to secure a position in the program, he'd doubted the young man's veracity, but after meeting secretly with several other interns of Pakistani lineage, they all confessed reluctantly to the scheme.

"Dr. Vipul, nice car you have there."

"Thank you. Handles terrifically. A bit self-indulgent I admit, but hey…"

Dan decided to get straight to the point. "You're selling positions in the program, I understand. How could you believe we wouldn't discover such outrageous behavior?"

Vipul looked down at his obscenely expensive shoes, unsure what to say next. Admit to it and get fired, probably, though there was a possibility that coming clean could generate a more lenient penalty. Denying it and having it proven would result in a most definite dismissal and possibly severe sanctions against him. He chose the first option.

"I apologize, Dr. Marchetti. I have no valid excuse. Saw an opportunity and took advantage of it. Unfortunately, this kind of action's commonplace in my home country."

"I don't know if that's true or not, but in any event, I expect your letter of resignation from our medical staff on my desk within the hour."

Vipul's brown eyes appeared frozen in a state of suspended disbelief, wide and fixed on the new CEO. "You can't be serious, sir!'

"Serious like a myocardial infarction." With that, Dan turned on his heels and walked briskly away, leaving the young physician stuck in place by superglue.

CHAPTER FORTY-FIVE

"A car theft ring? You have to be kidding me! Why would a physician be mixed up with such madness?" Dan sat on the edge of his bed, his Android on speaker, listening to his CFO recount a conversation he'd overheard in the hospital hallway. A young doctor, who he'd later identified as an intern after referring to the house staff pictures on one of the medical floors, had been vehemently discussing the arranged theft of his new Infiniti G35 with his lady friend, orchestrated by a GI attending in the hospital. She'd complained warily of the illegality of it all while he'd attempted to reassure her that the scheme was "foolproof" and was the answer to his financial difficulties brought on by his costly divorce.

"All right, I'll find out more in the morning. Jesus Christ, you can't make this stuff up!"

The next day, Marchetti called the intern, Bruce Talinowski, into his office to get his version.

"Bruce, one of my VPs overheard a conversation you were having with one of the ward clerks that concerned him greatly," Dan said.

"I don't understand." The man's beady brown eyes were wide open and fixed on the CEO.

"Did you arrange to have some business associates of Dr. Hank Van Patten steal your car in an attempt to collect insurance money?"

"What?" He blurted out loudly, his right leg now pumping up and down like a piston.

"I believe you heard me. I'd advise you to come clean now before you get in so deep that you'll be unable to extricate yourself. A disastrous path, I might add, that will lead to your personal and professional ruin."

Bruce attempted to maintain his composure, but as the gravity of his dilemma became clearer to him by the second, he erupted in uncontrollable sobbing.

"Margaret, would you please send for Dr. Hank Van Patten," Dan requested of his chief administrative secretary. A brief five minutes followed, though for Bruce Talinowski it felt like eternity. Van Patten soon stood in the doorway knocking quietly on the opened door frame.

"You sent for me, Dr. Marchetti?" He asked innocently, though his eyes darted back and forth between the CEO and the intern, Talinowski, who took great pains to avoid looking at the ringmaster.

"I did. Come in and close the door."

Hank denied any involvement, but later that week he was arrested while on walking rounds in the hospital for "car ringing," procuring cars and assigning them new VIN numbers. If convicted, a sizeable prison sentence undoubtedly would ensue. An exceptionally promising career had gone up in smoke.

***

As Dan was about to pass through the door to the CEO's suite of offices, he observed Dr. Carl Becker exiting the physician lounge directly across the hallway. He motioned for the plastic surgeon to enter his office. Marchetti remained determined that business as usual would no longer exist at his facility.

"Just need you for a few minutes."

"All right."

Once seated, Marchetti got right to the point. "Carl, I've received no less than five written complaints from patients of yours who you either examined as an outpatient in your office or while they were in the hospital where you consulted."

Carl sat up erect in the chair. "Oh? What was the gist of these letters?"

"Very simply, they all included copies of your bills with certain procedural charges listed that they all claimed were bogus ones. They asserted to a person that the procedures mentioned never took place then or at any time."

"Nonsense. These are uneducated, unsophisticated people who don't understand medical terms, medical instruments, or medical language."

"Really? One was a lawyer, one an accountant, one a schoolteacher and yes, two were blue-collar workers."

"My position's simple, Dr. Marchetti. I'm innocent."

"We're investigating this entire matter. For the time being, we're suspending your privileges here until we reach a conclusion."

"Fuck you. I'll simply take my services down the road. I'll resign from your staff. You'll receive my letter of resignation tomorrow and expect to hear from my lawyer in short order. Your comments are libelous and a pack of lies."

"I didn't reach a conclusion on the matter, as I stated, but if true, there's no place here for someone of such unethical behavior. Goodbye. I'd advise you not to do anything in such haste."

"Believe me, I know what I'm doing."

That remained to be seen.

***

The General didn't have a clue as to what this meeting was about. In any event, the CEO, Dr. Marchetti, had called him to his office to talk.

"Here to see Dr. Marchetti as requested," the General announced to one of the receptionists who worked in the President's office.

"He's running a bit late. Please make yourself comfortable in the meantime."

Fifteen minutes later, Marchetti's door opened, and he emerged, motioning for the taciturn urologist to enter his office.

"You know, I have a busy schedule too," he snarkily commented. His military background had trained him to always be on time.

"This won't take long," Dan answered back, a stern look on his tired face.

Having settled into the worn-looking leather chair behind his desk and the General ensconced in one of the two dark blue handsomely upholstered chairs parked in front of the wide desk, the CEO began.

"I'll get right to the point." Referring to his notes on his desk, "Last Tuesday you operated on a Samuel Rosen, did you not?" Without waiting for the answer, Dan continued. "I see you attempted to insert a penile implant to help reverse his erectile difficulties, yes?"

"I most certainly was," the General responded defensively, for now he knew the purpose of this meeting.

"Now, I've been told that your patient, while waiting to be brought into the operating room, complained of a 'crushing chest discomfort,' is that true?"

"Crushing, not really, but yes, chest pain, more like an ache."

"No, no, 'crushing' according to both the nurse's notes and the medical resident's notes as well, the one you called to help. 'Like an elephant sitting on top of my chest!' Couldn't be more classic for a MI, now, could it?" Dan paused long enough to clear his throat. "You must have also believed so because you asked the third-year medical resident what tests to order. To which he replied, a 'set of troponins and an EKG.' You ordered them, but according to the information gleaned from the chart and my sources, you didn't wait for the results before wheeling the patient into the operating room. Is that correct?"

"The surgery's a piece of cake, in and out."

"Piece of cake," Dan repeated sarcastically. "Except it wasn't. The patient cardiac arrested on the table. The anesthesia staff successfully resuscitated him and, by the way, the troponins were positive, and the EKG showed that the patient was in the midst of experiencing an anterior wall myocardial infarction—a heart attack." Dan removed his reading glasses rapidly, bristling in anger.

"Excuse me!" The General blurted out, his back stiffening.

"He sustained a fuckin' heart attack which put him at risk for sudden death. A premed student would know that. So, what happens? He cardiac arrests right there on the table while you continue, despite all of this, putting a piece of plastic in his penis. What kind of incompetent doctor ignores all those red flags?"

"I beg your pardon!" Again, the General responded haughtily, taken aback by Marchetti's tone and demeanor.

"Then, as if this wasn't egregious enough, you decide with the idiot anesthesiologist to continue this TOTALLY ELECTIVE procedure which, surprise, results in his once again cardiac arresting, for Christ's sake!"

With that, the General stood up, his eyes narrowed in fury, his fists clenched, and his posture ramrod-straight, unaware that his white lab coat had slid too far back in his neck region.

"I was a general in the Filipino Army, sir, a much-respected military man in my home country! You can't talk to me in such a disrespectful way."

Marchetti rose from his chair, moving swiftly to the front of his desk so that his nose was only inches from his counterpart.

"I don't give a rat's ass about all of that, Doctor! You're either too stupid to practice good medicine or so money-hungry that to lose a billable surgery goes against every safe medical instinct you may still have. But it really doesn't matter. Even though your own Chair of Surgery is too timid to take any action for this outrageous act and a whole litany of other questionable practices, I don't have such a problem. I hereby suspend your clinical privileges here and am reporting you to the State Medical Society. It's my absolute firm desire to see that you never practice your brand of medical care in our hospital again or State for that matter. DISMISSED, GENERAL!"

***

Marchetti pressed the metal plate on the hallway wall, allowing entrance to the surgeons' locker room. He was looking for Dr. Richard Robinson, the neurosurgeon reported to have alcohol on his breath by a scrub nurse and patient. Knowing he was scheduled to scrub in shortly to remove a glioblastoma multiforme, a highly malignant brain tumor, the nurse did the correct thing to head off a potentially catastrophic event. It was so unusual an occurrence for a colleague to signal such behavior, Marchetti would remind himself to seek her out for praise later. It was a courageous act to inform upon a physician who held such a powerful position. The truth was that Robinson, a man in his late forties, had far too many complications from his surgeries. His patients exhibited a particular propensity towards excessive bleeding that complicated their post-op recovery.

Dan sighted the athletic-looking surgeon changing into his pale green hospital scrubs in the corner of the room, facing an open locker where his street clothes hung, his shoes placed neatly below them. He was about to don white clogs on his feet, a favorite for surgeons, who'd often stand for six to ten hours at a time. He was scheduled momentarily to dissect around a tumor, attempting to leave as much healthy brain tissue as possible, thus limiting any neurological deficit.

"Dr. Robinson, do you have a few minutes?" Dan sat down astride the bench to directly confront the neurosurgeon.

"Oh, hello, sir. Of course. What can I do for you?"

The new CEO smelled the distinct aroma of alcohol in the air.

"Richard, do you think it advisable to drink alcohol on days you go to the operating room?" No beating around the bush—Marchetti always preferred the direct approach.

"No, I don't. I assume you smell something like alcohol now, prompting that rhetorical question? The smell comes from a very strong mouthwash that I use."

At that point, Dan produced an intoximeter which he'd grabbed from the ER before ascending the flight of stairs to the suite of operating rooms. Robinson laughed nervously, his embarrassment soon replaced by anger, which escalated by the second until the muscles in his face maintained almost a permanent state of contraction. Seething, he responded, "Contrary to what you'd believe, not all African Americans drink to excess and are lazy and irresponsible, Dr. Marchetti!"

"Don't obfuscate my message here. White, black, brown, or whatever, operating on anyone while under the influence is wrong and unacceptable. I seriously don't believe for one second you'd want a member of your family to be subjected to such dangerous behavior."

"My record's spotless, sir." He lost eye contact with that comment. Pushing the instrument away, he made it crystal clear that he wasn't going to allow himself to be tested, ignoring the obvious that his CEO had done his homework before confronting him.

"Firstly, your record, despite your younger age, is far from spotless. Though neurosurgeons are often the target of malpractice suits, the number of cases already filed against you to date exceed by a large margin the customary in both number and settlement dollars." Dan paused for effect. "What happened with Russell Cronenworth?"

"Excuse me?"

"The twenty-six-year-old man who's a quadriplegic now. The one you operated on six weeks ago. The one who filed a complaint that he smelled alcohol on your breath when you evaluated him in the Emergency Room after crashing his motorcycle."

"Wait, are you blaming me for his outcome? He'd been racing at over one-hundred miles per hour that evening with a friend, the idiot."

"That's correct. However, we received other complaints from his family after you informed them that the surgery had not gone particularly well. That there was a lot of bleeding, which eventually led to pressure exerted on the spinal cord, which you additionally failed to recognize during his immediate post-op period. This despite several worried calls from the Surgical ICU nursing staff. All these unfortunate incidents are documented. The family has retained counsel, I'm told."

Robinson seethed.

"Okay then, you're not going anywhere near the operating room now or until you get some help. I'll inform the Chief of Surgery immediately."

"No need. I'll operate down the block at Good Samaritan."

"We'll see about that, Richard."

The neurosurgeon galloped out the exit door, slamming the metal plate ferociously beforehand. He glanced back at the hospital CEO, who for his part stood his ground, his look of indignation melting away.

Leaning forward, Dan cautioned, "The work environment is sacrosanct and can only be occupied by committing to always wanting to do better by our patients, otherwise we sell them short and endanger their lives. Goddamn it, it's about caring."

This was the part of his job that he most disliked, but also, he felt strongly, why a physician-CEO of a hospital was so needed.

CHAPTER FORTY-SIX

"Let me play devil's advocate for a moment," Dominic offered up to one of his associates, still trying to make sense of why Dr. Marchetti acted nonplussed by his people letting him know that they made the Munchausen lawsuit disappear.

"First, those settlements are pre-tax dollars and can be crippling, especially to an industry with razor-thin net margins, if they're fortunate enough to be in the black. Plus, and this is a big one, CEOs of hospitals have no job security. None."

"Precisely. Precisely. Self-interest. You know, I recall reading about that scoundrel Avery Brundagel, who travelled to Hitler's Germany before the 1936 Olympic Games in Berlin. He went to register America's threat of pulling out of the Olympic Games if the Nazis didn't clean up their act. The Nazis in turn, knowing that Brundage was a successful builder, offered him the contract for the German Embassy in Washington DC, a huge edifice they'd envisioned. The *stronso* attested to their promise of good behavior and thus the threat of the boycott disappeared. The rest was history, Jesse Owens won four gold medals. No, self- interest is what this world's about and I'm certain Dr. Dan Marchetti's no different than everyone else. However, we'll need to ratchet up the pressure to work with us. As for the other physicians who gladly signed on, somewhere along the line their initial mission in medicine of doing 'good' was replaced by doing 'well.'"

***

"Dr. Marchetti, we appear to have received a ransomware attack," Gio said, approaching him in the hallway. He'd been on his way to the CEO's office when he happened to spot Marchetti at the elevator banks. Instead of calling out his name, which would've looked very unprofessional, he observed the floor that Marchetti exited, accessed the stairway, and caught up to him in short order.

"A ransomware attack, really?"

"Yes, sir."

"Show me now. I need to see this for myself."

"Let me do this in my office or in yours."

"Yours is closer, Gio?" Gio oversaw the IT system for the entire hospital.

"It is."

"Lead the way." It didn't take long to arrive at Gio's door, where he proceeded to make a beeline to his computer. It wasn't every day when the CEO of the entire hospital came to his "bunker."

There it was in black and white, though the ask, *Ten million dollars*, remained the only words that resonated in Marchetti's thoughts. Hospitals operated always on the thinnest of margins and his had been losing money the past few years. Furthermore, Marchetti was also aware that many if not most hospitals pay the amounts while some even pass it off as the "price of doing business."

Back in his office, the buzzer from his assistant sounded.

"Dr. Marchetti, the chief of Pediatrics is on the phone. She says it's an emergency." Marchetti had known Allison Sweeney for several years. Sure, the sixty-year-old dressed rather old-fashioned and carried herself in a matronly manner, but she rarely lost her cool.

"Yes, Allison, how can I help?"

"We have a three-year-old little girl who, after tonsil surgery, we fully expected to quickly treat for pain and dehydration and send home. The computer system that automatically calculated medicine doses wasn't working correctly and therefore gave her five times what was prescribed," she responded. "We need to wait hours while her body processes the overdose. "

"Allison, we're experiencing a cybersecurity threat and ransom attack. A cyberattack has probably taken down some or all the hospital's digital tools. I'm going to call an emergency meeting of all medical staff and close all nonessential services down until we develop a plan. From now on, all doses and clinical computations must be done by hand, the old-fashioned way, I'm afraid. Please notify your people now and I expect to meet with everyone within the hour."

"Oh my God. Surgeries are ongoing?"

"I'll address immediately." With that, Dan hung up the phone.

In times of crisis, some leaders rise to the occasion while others fold. Dan committed to being the former.

Ransomware, in which hackers extort companies and organizations by breaking into and often holding computers and files hostage, had become one of the toughest problems in cybersecurity and a threat to industries around the world. But it could be especially damaging when it hit hospitals, whether independent or chains, causing trickle-down damage to patient care in dangerous ways.

"Everyone, please quiet down." Marchetti raised his arms to accomplish just that. Most of the assemblage of over one-hundred managers and clinical leaders already had learned of the ransomware attack. News in a hospital travels almost at the same accelerated pace as medicine introduced through an IV.

"Okay, by now I believe that most of you have already learned of the cybersecurity attack that's taken place at our facility. I've converted my boardroom into a war room, so to speak, for the purpose of laser-focusing our attention on this existential threat. It appears at first glance that the cybersecurity incident was made possible when cybercriminals used a phishing email to trick an employee into installing malware on a computer on one of the medicine floors. There's a valuable lesson there. But nevertheless, I'm introducing to you Agent McIntosh of the FBI's rapid-response Cyber Action Team. Agent McIntosh…"

"Good morning." After briefly describing their unit and offering context to the overwhelming problem in healthcare cybersecurity, the agent described the five steps they'd employ immediately to prevent any injury or further damage. "One, start your incident response plan. It's critical to stop information from being stolen and repair your systems so a breach won't happen again. Two, preserve evidence. Three, contain the breach. Four, start incident-response management. And lastly," he leaned in on this one, his stern face accentuating this point, "investigate and fix your systems!" He strolled back and forth, weighing his next words carefully. "Ladies and gentlemen, for the time being, the hospital's functions almost assuredly will need to spiral down at once until our plan's enacted. Only activities related to those patients too sick to move elsewhere to other community hospitals must be dealt with solely by paper orders. Those whose dependence on machine-related actions need to be checked by as many individuals required to ensure safe action's always taken. I speak of ventilators and the like."

Marchetti listened intently, though he knew his hospital was in deep trouble in more ways than he could count.

This couldn't be related to Antonetti's people somehow, could it?

He tried to not let his mind go there, as there was simply too much to do presently.

CHAPTER FORTY-SEVEN

"What's wrong? She looks obtunded!" Dan shook Lauren by the shoulders but there was no response. Her entire body exhibited a tonic-clonic seizure, then the ER nurse attending her bounded in with the last labs drawn ten minutes earlier, her glucose dangerously low at twenty-eight.

Dan grabbed the piece of paper and immediately ordered, "Amp of D50, stat!" One of the meds given was a high-dose steroid and the resultant side-effect of producing diabetic sugars was being treated with an insulin drip. "Received too much insulin," Dan concluded, after analyzing the amount given already and over a short time frame.

"Oh my God, it began to run just a short while ago," her nurse exclaimed. She checked the IVAC and noticed the settings were distinctly different from the ones she'd set it on. She gasped.

"What is it, Denise?"

"Wrong settings."

"How the hell…" It hit him. The incident with the child a half hour before… The malware in the system was corrupting the medical devices, amongst other things.

After the D50 was given, Lauren's glucose level improved measurably.
***

Marchetti took the long way home that evening because he needed to think. He always found the monotony of driving conducive to exploring his thoughts, almost meditative as the road slipped away under the wheel. The big-ticket items, the surgeries, were all on hold, emergency ones shunted to other hospitals as were hundreds of their sickest patients. All too risky to attend to until the computer people got everything squared away. Even so, the fix would be expensive, no doubt, while paying the ransom money with no return on investment except the ability to continue. There was something so heinous and diabolical about the whole thing.

The persons doing this, or their loved ones, would undoubtedly seek out a hospital at some time, maybe even our own, should and when they fall seriously ill, the bastards.

Dan looked in his rearview mirror to see a dark Lincoln Continental approaching his BMW, the distance between the two vehicles quickly evaporating.

"Fuck, what the hell…"

His car was struck violently from behind, the force strong enough to push his car into the next lane, narrowly missing a SUV coming in the other direction.

That was clearly intentional. Why?

It happened so quick that he wasn't able to catch the license plate or the driver's face, other than a completely bald head as the crazed driver sped away.

***

"Dr. Marchetti, had you driven in such a way to have led to some road-rage incident?" Officer Harwood stared calmly at the concerned physician, whose right eye was swelling and becoming discolored. The collision had forced his head into the steering wheel of his car, but strangely enough, not sufficient to deploy the airbag.

Sitting in the front seat of the officer's squad car, Dan answered slowly, "I didn't think I cut anyone off, though to be honest, I might have, Officer. Anything's possible." He needed to think; he was not yet ready to complain to the police.

"You seem a bit preoccupied, sir. Now, you have no discernible alcohol level, but has there been any opiate or other narcotic use today or tonight? Sir?"

Dan's mind focused on a conversation he'd had the other day prior to the cyberattack, with one of the Board members.

"Son, you can't get anywhere in this life without being a team player. That's just a simple fact of life." He'd been talking about awarding a contract to a construction company with a spotty track record of safety and other assorted irregularities, to which Dan strenuously objected. The new CEO had sensed that this "advice" constituted a not-so-subtle message that applied to the contract pertaining to a refurbishing of the Emergency Room, amongst other hospital plans.

So, then he got a ransomware shitstorm followed by what appeared to him to be a deliberate automobile mishap. Coincidence?

Only a fool would believe that.

CHAPTER FORTY-EIGHT

"Dr. Marchetti, you need to get some fresh air. I'll call your cell should there be any changes," Amanda, the ICU head nurse, offered good-naturedly.

Dan gave one look back as he exited. Lauren was still unrousable despite having had her glucose levels normalized. Patting Amanda's shoulder, he quickly made his way down to his office to further contemplate the situation. By now, the two cases of clinical deterioration attributable to the ransomware attack appeared to represent the proverbial tip of the iceberg, as reports of all kinds of data theft and clinical mishaps were being reported throughout the healthcare system.

"But I have to prevent this entire matter from becoming intensely personal," he murmured to himself. This was not uncomplicated, especially since someone very dear to him was now unresponsive, and the other victim was a child for God's sake.

Besides, that incident on the road the other day and veiled warnings I've been receiving are overwhelming my thoughts. Profound trouble, close to home.

***

Taking a long break during the day, the exhausted CEO found himself ambling along the River Walk, recently constructed to encourage tourism with its trendy restaurants and cafes punctuating the landscape. Sitting down at a small empty table with only two chairs, Dan ordered a local IPA despite the hour of the day.

"Here you go, anything to go with it? We have some great wings," the overly made-up twenty-year-old offered, attempting to add to his bill.

"No thanks, maybe later."

She left dejectedly.

I know exactly the bastard who's behind this whole thing, and I swear to God, I will not flee, and I will not give in. Putting his doctors out of business was a very solid first step.

He'd have to be strategic, though.

CHAPTER FORTY-NINE

"We don't need to hurt you unless you don't agree to do what we say," the burly intruder warned, standing over a cot in the corner of the Salvation Army's accommodations for the homeless. The startled recipient of his threat looked around to see if anyone of authority could come to his aid. "Don't look around—you think any of these losers would come to your rescue should I decide to 'off' you right here and now?"

"No," Scott responded quickly, now sitting up in his pee-stained boxer shorts and torn dark blue Michigan University tee-shirt with faded yellow lettering, a 'hand-me-down' that he'd plucked from a garbage bin.

"God, you fuckin' stink. Do you even bathe at all?"

"Not much, I'm afraid. Today I will." The defensiveness in his voice was obvious.

"Listen and listen well." The man paused to light a cigarette, despite the NO SMOKING signs all around. "I'm about to offer you an opportunity." He smiled as he allowed the smoke to slowly exit the nostrils of his multi-fractured excuse for a nose. "We could use a man like you in our ranks, kind of like a foot soldier. That is, provided you cut down on the booze and do exactly what you're told."

Scott, ex-SEAL Team Six veteran and now a boozing, pill-popping PTSD sufferer, decided to play along.

"What would I be expected to do for you?"

"Well, you have a sister who's sweet on a doctor friend who just so happens to run that Sacred Heart Hospital down the block. Big shot. Dr. Dante Marchetti. Heard of him?"

"Why do you ask?"

Ignoring the question, the man continued, "You close with your sister?"

Scott decided to lie about their previously strained relationship, not wishing to close off his value before determining what it afforded him.

"Yes, yes, we are, though we fight like any other brother and sister."

"No kidding. My two older sisters think I'm wasting my life, but shit, even though our arguments can get nasty, I'd still defend them to my death. In fact," he chuckled out loud as he dropped his cigarette butt on the concrete floor and tapped it out, "I beat the crap out of the oldest one's boss after he fired her. She was rehired with an increase in pay." He smirked. "Now, get dressed and come with me, but take a damn shower first. Gonna buy you some real clothes and, for heaven's sake, run a toothbrush over those pearly whites."

Scott would keep playing along, at least for now.

***

"Going to get right to the point, Mr. Mason, because I'm that kind of guy," admonished Dominic Antonetti. "Your sister and the good doctor seem to be hot for each other. The good doctor's not been very appreciative of how we eliminated some of his troubles before they could seriously bite him in the ass, if you follow my drift. But he believes, I suppose, he's above it all." Dominic leaned forward so he was practically nose to nose with the target of his ire. "You need to get your sister to convince this stubborn character to do our bidding NOW."

Scott jumped in. "Or you'll hurt, or rather kill, both of them?"

"I see all those drugs haven't totally damaged your brain. Now get the hell out of here."

Scott knew that, even though he'd concluded that the only way out of this exceedingly deadbeat life would be to enter a rehab facility, these people would continue to underestimate him, a reality which could prove invaluable.

He stood up to leave, but not before he'd finished surveilling the suite of offices and what apparently served as the IT hub of their business enterprise. SEAL instincts and planning stuck with him despite the dulling effects of all the drugs he used to blunt his damn senses.

CHAPTER FIFTY

Scott managed to scrape enough money together to purchase a HP Envy x360, refurbished, of course, by working odd jobs given to him around the homeless shelter. Strange. Before going down his drug-addled past, he'd majored in computer engineering at a two-year college and developed quite a love affair with computer technology. Some would even describe him as a savant of sorts; he'd spend hours upon hours exploring, delving, pursuing areas far afield from his coursework. In particular, the entire subject of cybersecurity enthralled him.

Besides, reaching the excruciating lows of utter despair had been the complete antithesis of the type of individual the special forces bred and developed. Occupying his once fertile mind with challenging concepts and actions had to be his key to survival. Whispered conversation had alerted him that quite possibly there was a cybersecurity operation underway, involving the Sacred Heart Hospital and Dr. Dan Marchetti, its CEO. He'd become quite knowledgeable about all the combinations and permutations ransomware attacks could take. Or at least he had in the past. Perhaps he, Scott Mason, could be of some use, here on the inside.

Hackers would often use secure software such as proxy servers to hide their identity and funnel their communications through lots of different countries to evade detection.

Furthermore, the bombardment of the intended target's servers with junk traffic to distract whatever security staff a particular institution employed, if at all, was crucial during the ransomware installation.

***

Scott made his way into the "work" room that housed several computer terminals, blank magnetic striped cards, and other high-tech paraphernalia. Clearly the headquarters, so to speak, of their thinktank. He smirked to himself at the common misconception about ransomware attacks that they only involved "pay me to get your systems and data back" schemes—but these attacks had evolved into general extortion attacks. While ransom was still the main monetization angle for most attacks, in this case there existed a much more nefarious plan. Yes, attackers were also stealing sensitive data and threatening to disclose or sell it on the dark web or internet (often while holding onto it for later extortion attempts and future attacks). Sacred Heart Hospital was part of a broad chain of hospitals, so was threatened by this extortion attempt to allow for continuous access to data, long after the fix was applied. Dan was faced with the choice to pilfer Medicare and other insurers' data for hundreds of millions of dollars on a continuous basis, or else suffer the physical consequences to himself or to people he cared about.

The ransomware in the past pertained to basic cryptolocker-style attacks, first seen in 2013, that only affected a single computer at a time. These were supplanted by toolkits and sophisticated business models to enable human operators to target whole organizations, deliberately steal admin credentials, and maximize the threat of business damage to targeted organizations. Scott knew that ransomware operators often bought login credentials to organizations from other attack groups, rapidly turning what seemed like low-priority malware infections into significant business risks.

None of this would be beyond this criminal organization's capabilities, as this was no longer your father's underworld organization. This fact had become obvious to him. He also had become aware of the fealty the organization paid to the Russian Mafia in Brooklyn, having overheard an idle comment while waiting to see Antonetti.

Worse yet, Scott believed that the ransomware fix would only be applied when these guys had Marchetti on his knees and ready to do business. He'd try to help the embattled doctor who'd been so kind to him and his beloved sister.

If caught, he knew that he'd be executed on the spot.

CHAPTER FIFTY-ONE

"Dante, I believe I've fallen in love with you and, please, before you lecture me about our age difference, hear me out."

Dan tilted his head in a quizzical manner. "Okay."

Lauren fidgeted with her iPhone, not at all certain where to begin. "I've been searching my entire adult life, it seems, for a soulmate, someone who I could give myself to wholeheartedly without wondering if I was just incredibly needy or lonely for that matter. The effect of growing up devoid of any parental love per se can do quite a number on one's sense of belonging to someone…" Her voice trailed off.

Dan reached over and put his arm around her shoulder to draw her near.

"Lauren, that's just the point. Who am I to you?" As much as grabbing her, holding her tightly, and reciprocating would provide her what she needed, Dan couldn't help wondering whether her "love" for him was instead her need for him as a father figure. He decided to change the tenor of the conversation. "You deserve someone, Lauren, to build a complete life around with children and grow old together, not one way before the other."

"I'll let you in on a little secret. I always secretly wanted to adopt. Heaven knows, the world is made up of too many unwanted babies anyway. A child's special, no matter their origin. But…" Lauren placed both hands around the back of his neck and clasped them together while Dante stared at the ground. Unable to hold back any further, she hungrily reached for his mouth and kissed his lips until the force of it hurt. She stopped abruptly and realized that her fervor wasn't being reciprocated. It was time to go.

CHAPTER FIFTY-TWO

Before Scott opened his response from 23 and Me, he reflected on how far he'd come in his rehab program. The constant refrain of "people, place, purpose, and perseverance," which almost drove him to distraction, had taken hold somehow. This DNA test which his former self would never have bothered with, he took to satisfy a ridiculous curiosity, ninety-nine percent certain there would be no match with Dr. Marchetti, or anyone else for that matter. But it made sense to satisfy himself that he'd fully dealt with his past before embarking on the future. After all, Lauren's had been negative, so as her fraternal twin, how could he be positive and her negative? But maybe, just maybe, his biological physician father was searching for them and, mistakes happened. Ironically, here he was, a grown man, still craving a connection with his biologic father despite the odds being so infinitesimally low. Besides, the chances were that, should he be found, he'd want absolutely no connection to them anyway. In any event, spending the few dollars Scott made on a used computer and a lab test was infinitely more positive than incapacitating drugs. Maybe this time he'd turned the corner.

Scott immediately accessed the DNA relatives' tool, the one detail he genuinely cared about. The results so shocked him that he found himself overcome with emotion, this ex-SEAL Team Six member who used to be tough as nails. A match with Dante Marchetti, MD! But how could this be? Lauren's failed to show the same result. How reliable were these tests? Scott needed answers before the day was out.

Otherwise, he risked losing his mind then and there.
***

"I have some really wild news for you Laur…" Scott said, after his sister had opened her door to let her wayward brother into her home.

"You do?" She interrupted enthusiastically. "Been wanting to reach out to you several times since returning from the hospital a month ago. Didn't want to disturb your progress in rehab, though."

They hugged, his embrace firmer and longer this time.

"Looks like it's made all the difference. Am I correct?" She asked rhetorically. He'd gained weight and started to work out—gone was that hospital pallor, replaced by a slight sunburn. "Been outside, I see?

"Running, lifting every day now." Just like during his Navy SEAL days.

Bypassing any further small talk, Scott led his sister to the sofa, as what he was about to say would come as quite a shock. "Listen, I've got something important to share." He paused, tears welling in his dark brown eyes. "A *chimera*. Ever heard of it?"

"A vegetable? A car?" She paused when her brother stared at her. "I don't have a clue." She giggled nervously.

Scott reached for a letter from an opened envelope which he'd held in his right hand. Lauren made out an official-looking report contained in a full-page, computer-generated document with the return address on the envelope, 23 and Me.

Lauren's body tensed and her heart raced. She knew immediately that the contents of his letter might very well change their lives dramatically, though she was getting far ahead of herself.

"In genetics, an organism or tissue that contains at least two different sets of DNA, most often originating from the fusion of as many different zygotes."

"What're you reading me? Am I supposed to be impressed?" She asked nervously. She knew her brother was intelligent and had been extremely well-read before his life devolved into drugs.

Scott continued undeterred, so Lauren decided to let him finish before interrupting again.

"In 1953, a human chimera was reported in the *British Medical Journal*. A woman was found to have blood containing two different blood types. Apparently, this resulted from her twin brother's cells living in her body. A 1996 study found that such blood group chimerism's not rare. In 2018, a chimera was found in Korean triplets."

"Scott, Scott, I'm confused, help me out here. Are you implying that our mother was pregnant with triplets, we survived, and one of us carries that individual's DNA?"

"Yes, exactly. Perhaps the answer resides in the fact that we were in fact triplets and our sibling died in the womb. I met with a geneticist at the hospital who suggested this explanation."

There it was, unimaginable proof that Dr. Dante Marchetti was the semen donor that impregnated their late mother. Their father. That would also explain his twin sister's results showing the contrary.

"Lauren, for Christ's sakes, do you understand what this all means? Dr. Dante Marchetti's our father!" He exclaimed.

The brother and sister hugged ferociously, not wanting to let go out of fear that doing so would lead to a freefall into their new reality without a rope to grab onto. Their world had just been turned upside down. Missing out on all those years of celebrating Mother's and Father's days, birthday parties, parents watching their dance recitals or T-ball games, and on and on and on. But especially the feeling of *worthlessness* which had become like a functionless third leg, always present but serving no useful purpose. Anytime Lauren felt proud of an accomplishment, like putting herself through college and law school, only to trip over this cursed appendage. Or her brother seeking refuge in pills and the like when he desperately needed a father to help him navigate through his feelings of worthlessness. Even at an older age.

Finally releasing each other, Scott spoke first.

"It's strange. I knew, deep down, I knew the truth. When I met him the first time in the hospital, I can't explain it, but a strange feeling overcame me."

"How do you mean?" Lauren tilted her head, her long hair shifting to that side. If only her instincts had saved her from thinking of Marchetti in a sexual way.

"Like, like I've seen that movie before, like in in a dream."

"A dream that conjured up our father's face as it is today?"

"Exactly. You too?"

"Yes, but in my dreams, he looked exactly like you, my brother."

"Not surprising. But I think God was showing me what our dad looked like in case I saw him in a crowd, in a supermarket, in a church."

Lauren held her brother's hands in her own. "What do we do, let him know what we've learned?"

"Of course."

"But when, and what if it doesn't go well? Wouldn't that be more devastating?" Lauren fretted.

For Lauren, it presented an even more horrifying problem. She had romantic feelings emerging for this man, a man who now turned out to be her own father. The thought made her want to cry out in revulsion.

"Scott, I suppose this comes as no shock to you that for the first time in such a long time, I started to feel a desire for intimacy again. Talk about the 'ick factor.' Jesus, Mary, and Joseph!" They both laughed awkwardly at the absurdity of it all.

CHAPTER FIFTY-THREE

Later that evening, as Scott and Lauren sat at a sushi bar for dinner, Lauren remarked, "This is too much to fathom all at once." Her eyes glistened, she caught herself.

"Lauren, the mob tried to strong-arm me awhile back to have you talk to Dan Marchetti about 'playing ball.' I chose not to speak a word of it to you."

"Did they threaten you?"

Scott smiled. "Doesn't work with me."

"An FBI agent informed Dan that his life could be threatened by Russian mobsters, who've lost their patience with this Dominic Antonetti, the hospital Chairman of the Board and mobster."

"Please fill me in. I'm a little lost here."

Lauren described all that Dan had confided in her.

"Let me get this straight. We've spent our entire lives wanting to meet our biological father. Now that we've made such a miraculous discovery, his life and yours are in danger?"

Not if I can help it! It's time to stare down the wolf, Goddammit.

The "wolf" was a metaphor used during SEAL training for fear, all the deeply engrained negative emotions that held one back. Staring down the wolf was crucial to be able to unlock massive potential.

Eliminate those responsible for endangering the lives of the two most important people in his life.

***

But first, there was the matter of the ransomware attack at Sacred Heart Hospital. Scott worked feverishly, for he knew that while there were tens of thousands of ransomware variants and techniques to evade defense and detection, there were only a handful of encryption methods. Furthermore, the only way to decrypt ransomware without paying for the private keys was to obtain copies of the original files' encryption keys. This was exactly what he was looking for, but he had to work quickly for several reasons. Not the least being that if found here at Antonetti's offices, there wouldn't be a single plausible excuse for his presence in this room.

The proprietary and patented key extraction technology (SKI-Session Key Intercept) he stole online automatically detected encryption processes running in applications and in real time and monitored those code segments to intercept copies of the ransom keys. It was time to work expeditiously, but it was time that was in short supply.

***

Dan thought he'd stop at Enzo's Pizzeria and pick up a few slices for dinner before going home. Their thin crusted pies with basil and tomato sauce were his favorite, but while parking, Marchetti's sightline caught a familiar face at one of the high-end restaurants in town, Chef Tommy's. It was none other than Lauren Mason, amiably chatting with a youngish man in a dark suit, with a shaved head and very fit-looking. They were engaged in a clearly friendly, animated conversation. Maybe it was someone from work, another lawyer perhaps. What he felt deep within was difficult to describe, although part of it was the sense of joy in witnessing Lauren reaching out to others.

The thought of pizza, which he'd previously craved, became a non-issue, so he quickly decided to leave his parking place, concluding that spying one more second was truly beneath him.

Perhaps he needed to explore the dating world more aggressively or be destined to spend his days alone, without that special someone who could make his pulse quicken, monopolize his thoughts, and end that gnawing, debilitating sense of feeling so alone?

Without warning, a harsh rapping sounded on the driver's closed window, loud enough for bystanders to stop parading by to take note but barely loud enough to break the intended target's almost trance-like train of thought.

"Dante, Dante, lower your window. We need to talk." Lauren stood there; her face twisted in anguish. "Can I sit with you for a moment?"

Before he could open his mouth, Lauren came around his Subaru and plopped herself down in the passenger seat.

"Dan, I've tried to talk with you for a while now," she said earnestly.

"Oh?"

When she saw him in the parking lot, Lauren felt it necessary to reveal to him what she'd learned about their rare DNA anomaly. But now, in the moment, she froze. What if he rejected the truth and fled? Another abandonment would most assuredly devastate her very soul.

"Have I done something to anger you?" He asked when she said nothing.

She could've kicked herself for failing to reveal their discovery.

But could he possibly comprehend the longing I—we—have felt to know something, anything of the individual who partnered to create us? He'll need to know, but not right now.

"Of course not."

"I didn't mean to spy, just here to pick up a slice of pizza."

"Sounds great. Do you mind if I join you?"

"No, not at all, that would be nice."

CHAPTER FIFTY-FOUR

"How the fuck did this happen?" Asked Ivan Popov, the *Pakhan* of the Brighton Beach Russian mafia, his fist pounding on his mahogany desk in his office. Word had gotten to him that Antonetti's people had their ransomware attack thwarted, even though it was routed through servers in foreign countries to prevent a direct trace by law enforcement.

"I've heard some talk about sabotage within their organization. What did the camera show, who did this?" Popov inquired.

"Any images the cameras might've detected were erased, so we have no physical evidence to locate the bastard who managed this," came the reply.

"Antonetti's on borrowed time. He's unable to run his organization effectively, the *mudak*."

***

"Lauren, the results of the biopsy are back." Marchetti removed his reading glasses and rubbed his tired eyes more vigorously than was necessary.

"It's bad, isn't it? Cancer?" Lauren asked very meekly.

"No, no, no," he answered immediately, not at all wanting his patient to go down that rabbit hole. "There's inflammation involving the small veins called 'venules,' which appears to be what's causing you such pain. For the time being, we're labeling your problem as 'IgG4-related disease.'"

"I'm confused."

"The name doesn't matter; it's not cancer and is treatable. We'll continue with the strong medicine called Rituximab."

"Will this medicine eventually cure me?"

"Tough to say. Let's take it one day at a time, shall we?"

Lauren cried softly while reaching for Marchetti's hand. "Thank you for staying involved, trying to help…"

***

Two weeks later, Lauren met with her rheumatologist, Dr. Weitzman, a diminutive man in his early forties with a plaid bow tie and horn-rimmed black glasses.

"The repeat MRI of your brain after an additional two weeks of treatment, Lauren, is unfortunately showing a worsening of the abnormalities instead of an improvement." The specialist's face registered just enough concern, but he was cautious not to send his patient into a panic.

"Not surprised. Frankly, I haven't been feeling a whole lot better. Plus, I've been seeing double of everything."

"That's because the nerves supplying the muscles that control the eye movements have been affected as well. Now, certain lab tests have come back positive consistent with still another disorder called granulomatosis with polyangiitis, whose therapy calls for this same medicine plus another. Now, I know this is a lot to hear, but we'll get you better. Promise."

"From your mouth to God's ears."

"Just asking you to hang in there a while longer. Dr. Marchetti and I will not stop until we make you better."

God, don't let them become liars.

CHAPTER FIFTY-FIVE

The retrieval of some spinal fluid failed to reveal any sign of infection, either common ones or unusual pathogens like tuberculosis or fungal organisms.

"Dr. Pearlmutter, I have a patient who's going to need a biopsy of her meninges." These were the coverings of the brain; Dan was fortunate that they punched him directly through to the neurosurgeon, a diffident but extremely capable person.

"I see. Tell me about her."

Marchetti proceeded to explain the specifics of Lauren's case to the Chief of Neurosurgery at his hospital. It was an unusual request, but one that was clearly indicated in this strange case and further made necessary since high dose steroids had failed to alleviate her facial pain and debilitating headaches.

"I can schedule her tomorrow. Is that soon enough?"

"Perfect." Now to explain to the patient.

"Lauren," he addressed his suffering patient, who was now swaddled with cold compresses placed on her head, the hospital room darkened for obvious reasons despite the area outside being bathed in sunshine. "We're going to need a biopsy to retrieve some tissue from the covering over your brain in order to acquire a better handle on what's causing all this pain."

"Oh God…" She hesitated. "Do what you have to do… I can't go on like this, Dan."

"Tomorrow, then."

His patient vomited into the plastic basin lying by her head. "I want to die."

Dan grabbed her free hand firmly and held it, and though he would feel compelled to do so with any other patient, this one was different.

There had always existed a connection, an invisible cord that they shared.

***

Lauren experienced a momentary respite but sadly it was to last a mere forty-eight hours.

"Dan. I can't hear anything out of my right ear. I'm... I'm going deaf. Oh my God!"

Marchetti maneuvered around the gurney in the Emergency Room to put himself in a better position to complete a full neurological exam once again on his patient. What became clear soon enough was that, with her hearing indeed lost in one ear and her tongue deviated to one side, the pressure in her brain had increased substantially. Taking a moment to apply a gentle squeeze to his sobbing patient's arm, Marchetti wasted little time contacting the neurosurgeon again.

"Dr. Pearlmutter, Dan Marchetti here, I'm here with Lauren Mason whose hypoglossal and auditory nerves are out on the right side. I ordered a stat CT but I believe her ICP is elevated and she'll need a shunt." ICP referred to intracranial pressure.

"Okay, will be down shortly and if confirmed, I'll take her immediately to the OR."

The next day the shunt was successfully placed, reducing the pressure within the brain to normal levels.

Lauren seemed to embody the words, "Death by a thousand cuts."

CHAPTER FIFTY-SIX

"How do you feel now," Marchetti took a moment to peer at his EMR, "two months after the shunt and treatments?"

"Pretty good, I must confess, pretty damn good."

"I'm glad." After an exam to confirm what he already knew, Marchetti continued, "Well, you are one very unusual woman with a very unusual illness. We're all unanimous in the final naming of this complication, an entity entitled 'Pachymeningitis.'"

"Pachy? Like pachyderm, an elephant?"

"No, no," Marchetti laughed. "It's a disease that checks every box, including masquerading as the illnesses we previously thought you suffered from. It's a chronic inflammatory state that is not, I repeat not, from cancer and infection. I also believe your birth mother might have suffered from this as well."

"You deduced this from talking with my aunt?"

"Yes, she was helpful. She also told me that motherhood was the one thing your mom always wanted, above all else." Dan smiled warmly.

"Yes, I know." Tears trickled down her cheeks. "Now, you see what you've done, Dr. Dan Marchetti, you've made me cry!"

Dan reached for her hands and held them in his probably longer than he should have, but it was like an invisible force made him unable to separate. The simple truth was exposing itself; a strong bond was formed between the two.

***

Dan's words of encouragement awhile back continued to reverberate in Scott's thoughts until finally when he awoke one morning, he searched for his SEAL Team workout manual. The six-week regimen detailed within was guaranteed to whip his body into the type of shape that would make him, if not combat ready, at least in shape to accomplish what he needed to do. Included were long-distance workouts for jogging and swimming, high intensity for both, interval workouts, strength training for upper and lower body, a flexibility routine, and lastly, injury prevention drills. The interval cardio workouts alternating short intense bursts of energy proved to be the most arduous for him. Scott took pains to follow the optimal ratio of work to rest being 1:2 to 1:2.5, which meant that for every minute he would sprint or swim, he would rest for two to two and a half minutes. After only two weeks, he felt himself getting stronger, tighter, and leaner.

    ***

Dominic Antonetti chain-smoked after finishing his last cup of coffee that morning. He was to chair a meeting in his conference room shortly involving six contemporaries, all highly educated made men whose knowledge of the healthcare industry rivaled his own and whose education included three law degrees, two graduates of the Wharton School of Business, and one physician, Dr. Angelo Capriati. This was no longer your father's underworld.

"They're ready for you, sir," Alicia, his assistant informed him. "There's a carafe of coffee and croissants already there. If you need anything else, please let me know."

"Thanks, Alicia."

With that, he opened the door to his office, which led directly to the conference room. After exchanging pleasantries, he sat down and motioned for everyone to bring their refreshments to the exquisitely constructed Ranier Daumiller conference table and sit.

"Gentlemen, today we need to finalize the details for Bellecon Associates, our Jersey-based company whose main business is arranging and managing group medical, dental, and optical programs for employers and unions. We've developed quite an extensive network of healthcare providers in addition."

"How are the fees structured, Dominic?" Giuseppe Contadina, an extremely well-dressed man in his late fifties with a three-piece suit, purple pocket square, and blue-rimmed glasses, inquired politely.

"The companies and unions pay a fixed annual fee for each patient in the program and additional fees come from the providers."

"How do our organizations do in the final analysis?" Contadina countered immediately.

"Our fees should reflect our earnest efforts and come directly from the providers for managerial services. We lean on the plan administrators to approve the costs and all extra money snapped up is divided amongst our partners. But I have to say, the Medicare scamming, for want of a better word, represents a sizeable opportunity whose ceilings are unlimited, quite frankly. One of the best parts of all this is that we rarely have to settle a debt or silence a witness unless absolutely necessary. After all, we're gentlemen compared to those Russian animals." They all shook their head in unison. Theirs was a cleaner, tidier way of doing business.

"*Siamo d'accordo.*"

CHAPTER FIFTY-SEVEN

"As stated on another occasion, in this time of drastically reduced reimbursements, unfunded mandates for healthcare institutions, and the devastating financial debacle of the Covid pandemic, we're facing a 20-million-dollar shortfall this year to date."

"I'm aware, Dominic," Dan responded tersely during his weekly meeting with the Chairman.

"We went ahead with contracting the Bellecon consultants, who'll help us right-size and get our financial house in order, mission critical."

The treacherous waters Dan feared earlier were shark-infested for certain.

***

Dan tossed and turned, trying to welcome a good night's sleep but unable to extricate his mind from his troubles at hand. There was the Chairman of the Board seemingly usurping his new role right from the start by presenting a plan hatched beforehand that confounded him. Finally concluding that sleep was a no-show, Dan made his way over to his computer.

Before long, he had in front of him the Sacred Heart Hospital's homepage, which he read quickly. The usual promo extolling their tremendous healthcare experience and smorgasbord of services appeared at once. Clicking on the 'Team' section, he recorded the names, their administrative roles, and their backgrounds. He'd need to find out more about these select group of board members with whom his Chairman of the Board was so enamored. It was unsettling to feel beholden to someone who'd had the final say on his appointment. One thing Dan knew for certain—there was no place in his life for *quid pro quos*.

***

"Dr. Marchetti, Agent Jackson of the task force here. Sir, as you know, the cybersecurity threat came and went with no explicable reason. No ransom was paid, a rare event indeed. Uncharacteristic, I might add, as these attacks generally play out."

"I don't understand."

"Something appears to have happened on their end. Cold feet? Doubt it. Internal dissention, maybe. We're not at all looking this gift horse in the mouth and are quickly and effectively doing our best to safeguard your hospital as best we can from here on out."

"Care to hazard a guess as to what happened there to put a halt to everything?" Dan pursued any possible answer.

"Like I intimated, either someone had a severe case of regrets, or you have a 'friend' on the inside. No other explanation I can contemplate, Doctor."

These people never regret anything. A friend on the inside, then?

CHAPTER FIFTY-EIGHT

Sitting barely awake at her kitchen table, coffee mug in hand, Lauren admired how her remodeled room provided exactly the feel of a country kitchen she'd always desired. Open, lots of sunshine, a focus on natural materials, lightly stained wooden tables and chairs, matching cabinets with built-in organizers and pullout shelves. The colors featured all kinds of shades of gray or white, which although it cost plenty, screamed out the words "comfortable" and "cozy."

Reflecting on the past few months, the young lawyer reveled in the good fortune she enjoyed, her good health having returned.

Scanning the butcher block countertop, her eyes spotted a mason jar containing home-preserved green beans and tomatoes given to her by a grateful client whose case she'd successfully handled. It had been a tax code infringement that appeared on the surface to be prosecutorial overreach after multiple futile attempts to make more serious charges stick with a grand jury. The client was a Russian gentleman who presented himself as an everyday businessman with a legitimate trucking concern. Or so it would appear to be on the surface, though her inspection only involved some tax code questions.

Gifts, however, were not uncommonly bestowed upon her as a sign of appreciation for working demanding hours on her client's behalf. Clients almost always fixated on the exorbitant fees charged, which she had to admit were hard to justify. However, on occasion, gifts were bestowed upon her, like the stunning flowers and expensive theatre tickets that had been left one day at the front desk for her. This thanks to a homeowner who she'd successfully represented against an environmental company, one that tested her home and determined it to be a smorgasbord of indoor pollutants, including the deadly mycotoxin *Stachybotrys chartarum*. Their report, once filed, had caused her house to lose half of its value, forcing her to move the property in essentially what amounted to a fire sale. The loss had amounted to hundreds of thousands of dollars and caused tremendous anxiety and depression for this single mother. The defendant, Environmental Housecall Inc., a multibillion-dollar enterprise whose practices were now being exposed to the light of day by lawyers such as Lauren, had agreed reluctantly to an out-of-court settlement. Their Chief Counsel had begun his company's defense against claims of malfeasance, only to lose all pretense at civility when he lambasted her client's motives and character.

Lauren had no reason to believe at that time that Dominic Antonetti, who so viciously verbally assaulted her client, had anything to do with Dan and the Sacred Heart Hospital.

It was already mid-morning on her day off, and Lauren felt overwhelmed by hunger, leading her to open the mason jar to taste the vegetables within. Tomatoes she adored, though green beans represented an "evil weed," a term Newman from *Seinfeld* made famous when referring to broccoli. The food tasted sharp, though she enjoyed the tomatoes, which she placed on top of a toasted piece of wholewheat bread spread with a thin layer of pesto. Preserving foods was one of the few pleasant reminders of her time spent with her aunt, whose drinking and ranting about several life's cruel tricks plagued their years together.

After placing her breakfast dish and utensils in the dishwasher, Lauren retired to the living room to read the local paper, but found her eyelids heavy, despite eight hours of unquestionably restful sleep the night before. Though it was unusual for her to nap during the day, she quietly drifted off into a deep sleep, deciding not to fight the urge despite her long list of errands. They'd just have to wait.

A few hours passed before she was woken abruptly by her cellphone. Lauren noted her friend Cleo's name on her Android and started to greet her, "Hell…Ceeeyooo," but she was shocked to hear her words come out slurred, even garbled.

"Lauren, did I wake you?" Cleo inquired rather matter-of-factly, not suspecting that anything was amiss. Just a sleepy friend or a hungover one. However, when her bestie continued to fail at making herself understood, she became alarmed. "I'll be right over." She debated whether to call an ambulance first, but decided to go there directly since it was only a five-minute drive.

Upon entering the house and finding Lauren unrousable, only then did she know that something was terribly wrong. Cleo whisked her off herself to the Emergency Room without wasting time waiting for an ambulance.

"We need to determine when her speech became abnormal," the ER doctor inquired of both the patient and Cleo, though the latter could only describe the timing of the phone call. Lauren, now awake, was able to write on paper that she awoke like this after falling asleep two hours before, precisely.

Acute stroke was a possibility and strong blood thinning medication had to be considered. But someone her age especially would have other possibilities in her differential diagnosis list. Looking at her online medical record, this could be a result of her ongoing illness. All were very serious possibilities.

CHAPTER FIFTY-NINE

By now the neurologist on call had been paged, and fortuitously, Gary Blanchfield had been next door evaluating an eighty-six-year-old woman with a stroke, so he arrived on the scene within ten minutes.

Lauren managed to declare that she was also having trouble chewing, blurry vision in both eyes, and had trouble shuffling to her friend's car, besides feeling extremely weak.

"Ms. Mason, do you use illegal drugs of any kind?" Blanchfield stared at his patient's face, undoubtedly also watching her body language to shed some light on her condition.

Black tar heroin and cocaine could produce this picture.

Lauren shook her head, annoyed by the question, though she understood why it was asked.

"I'm going to do a drug screen, nevertheless. You'd be surprised at the number of people who don't tell the truth under these circumstances," he offered impoliticly. By now, Lauren was busy texting Dante while deep down, she feared an exacerbation of her previous inflammatory condition.

I thought it'd been left in my rearview mirror.
***

"CAT scan of her head was totally normal. Her tox screen came back negative, as did her alcohol level. Does she drink at all, Dan?" Blanchfield inquired of his colleague.

"A glass of wine here and there. Also, her inflammatory markers are negligible, so I don't think this picture is due to her previously diagnosed autoimmune process."

"Blood pressure has stayed extremely high, 200 systolic. Worrisome. Getting loaded with IV Labetalol, thiamine and dextrose, aspirin, simvastatin."

"What does your gut tell you, Gary?" Dan braced for his answer.

"Myasthenia gravis, multiple sclerosis, Wernicke's, or even botulinum poisoning, which would be rarer than rare. Has she gotten any cosmetic treatment or chronic headache treatment with botox that you know of?"

Dan smirked, "Lauren doesn't believe in such stuff and no headache issue to date."

Of course, botulinum toxin can be seen in other scenarios.

***

Dan took Lauren's keys from his pocket with no need to disarm the security system since her friend Cleo had hurriedly scooped her up in her car and driven her to the hospital. The intensely worried and curious physician was on a mission, as the possible diagnosis of botulinum toxicity appeared to represent a distinct possibility. Antibodies for myasthenia gravis and other entities had come back negative and botulism loomed large in his mind. But how and why?

Botulinum neurotoxin serotype A was the most toxic substance known to man, with an estimated lethal dose of 120 nanograms—a grain of sugar weighs approximately 625,000 nanograms. This was within the realm of possibility should someone procure one to two 100-unit vials of commercially available Botox product.

Dan was struck by the fastidious surroundings as every pillow was arranged perfectly, countertops unencumbered and pristine, sink immaculate, and so on. He couldn't help thinking about some of the common beliefs as to why individuals who have such tendencies behaved this way. One addressed routine childhood triggers, specifically so-called "reassurance-seeking" behavior. To find that reassurance in other things, to trust the world not to hurt them, and finally, to let go of the scared kid who needs so badly to feel safe. That was the Lauren he'd so come to know.

Scanning the room for any clue, he opened the refrigerator, whose items also were arranged in an ordered system with actual labels. Under "Surprise" on a shelf with a singular item was a canning jar with green beans and tomatoes.

***

"Lauren, I found a mason jar in your home today that contained green beans and tomatoes. Did you ingest some of them and, if so, when?" Dan asked, facing his patient, who sat up in a lounge chair in her hospital room. Since she still had difficulty making herself understood, she motioned for the pad and pen by her nightstand. Marchetti complied.

What day is today? She scribbled, her youthful face registering consternation at her loss of time, not place.

"Tuesday, the fifth of June."

With that helpful information, she wrote, *Four days ago.*

"From where did you obtain this jar?"

Lauren thought for an appreciable amount of time but only responded with a *?*

"You don't recall?" He asked disappointedly.

She shook her head.

"Try to remember. It's important, for several reasons."

Lauren acknowledged his request but peered at the man who'd become so important in her life with a quizzical stare.

"The contents were sent to the Public Health Department, and guess what? The green beans tested positive for botulinum toxin A." Dan let that information settle.

Lauren clearly comprehended the surprising news, now holding both palms skyward as if to say, "How come?" The news needed a few moments to register.

It was certainly a rare but not unknown occurrence in these kinds of jars.

"I'm now administering botulism antitoxin A. We'll need to wait to allow the medicine to work, Lauren. Please keep the faith. This issue is not, I repeat, not related to your inflammatory condition," he insisted. The toxin was made most often by *Clostridium botulinum* bacteria. Improperly canned, preserved, or fermented foods can provide the right conditions for the bacteria to manufacture the toxin.

Did this occur naturally or was it added to the jar to make it appear that way? Either way it was disturbing, though the latter thought was also maddening.

CHAPTER SIXTY

Weeks passed and finally Lauren was weaned from supplemental oxygen, no longer requiring a skilled nursing facility, and essentially returned to a normal state, albeit having lost over twenty pounds and tremendous stamina. She resumed her duties as a lawyer part-time for the next six weeks.

The research she did on botulism became an obsession, however. To her astonishment, she learned that the conditions that enable the spore-forming bacillus are rarely achieved in the human intestinal tract, which would explain why only thirty-five cases exist each year, more or less, in the United States. The neurotoxins must then travel through the blood to the peripheral nerve system. The brain's spared because the poison is too large to cross through the barrier to the brain.

Meanwhile, Dan once again studied Lauren's medical records for any additional clues that could shed light on her unusual condition. Botulism's so extremely rare and how could someone, anyone be so resourceful as to create the ideal conditions for the toxin to be produced during a canning procedure and ensure that kind of lethal poisoning? Unless...

Someone added the commercial product used legally in clinical medicine to the vegetables to create the appearance that the powerful neurotoxin emanated from the canning process. But why go to such great lengths?

***

Dominic awaited his turn to tee off. The sun was radiant, the grass had been freshly mowed, and the greens had never been in such exquisite condition, albeit quite brisk, at his extremely exclusive country club in Bergen County. The Sun Valley had only 460 members and was known for only admitting highly successful businessmen with the initiation fee at half a million dollars.

"You're up, Dominic!" Exclaimed Sid Rosenthal, a golfing buddy of over ten years, both men having joined around the same time.

Dominic removed a tee and Titleist golf ball from his pants pocket and leaned over to set the tee in the ground when he felt overwhelmingly lightheaded and fell to his knees. The vertigo he experienced caused him to throw up his recently ingested Cobb's salad on the tee box, which embarrassed this proud man to no end. Trying to stand only made things worse, as he staggered like a drunken sailor until he voluntarily sought the safety of the ground or face-plant directly onto the expensive sod.

"Call an ambulance!" He screamed as his instincts told him that he could be having a stroke. The starter had already summoned the EMS, which arrived within five minutes, transporting him to Sacred Heart Hospital's Emergency Room before too much time had elapsed.

***

"Been vomiting over and over again the past few days," Antonetti lamented to the Emergency Room physician. No sooner did those anguished words come from his mouth did he grab for the emesis basin and return the water he'd just forced down.

"How many times have you vomited each day and has there been any blood in the vomitus?" The tall, freckled doctor inquired matter-of-factly.

The patient, too nauseated to respond verbally, shook his head negatively to the blood question and held up the five fingers of his left hand (his right one being busy holding the basin).

"I see. I'm going to replace your fluids with an IV, give you something for the nausea, and order some tests. Probably a garden-variety gastroenteritis, nothing more."

With that, he turned and exited the bay in his ER while Dominic Antonetti could only shake his head to indicate his understanding. Even this slight movement initiated another bout of retching.

***

Due to Antonetti's status as Chairman of the Board, Dan had been notified to check in on his VIP patient. He reluctantly did so, though his dislike for this man for good reason had grown exponentially. A few hours later, Marchetti returned after having examined the lab results, which had alarmed him.

"Mr. Antonetti, are you a diabetic?"

"Not that I'm aware of, Doctor?" Dominic responded, a decided look of dismay on his beleaguered face. "Is that what my lab work shows?"

"Your sugars are elevated, but sometimes that can occur when the body's stressed, though quite possibly you are diabetic. Does it run in the family?"

Antonetti shook his head affirmatively, his disheveled hair plastered to his scalp. "Both sides, unfortunately."

"All your labs are out of whack, as a matter of fact. This still may be a simple GI bug, maybe norovirus, maybe a bacteria. However, I'll need to send a stool sample for culture. In any event, I'm going to send you home on some medicine to follow up with your primary care doc."

The next day, Dominic dutifully complied and made an appointment with his internist. Each day he felt sicker and more debilitated.

"Dr. Bauman, it's been two weeks and I still feel like shit. I knew we shouldn't have visited my wife's uncle's farm in Australia."

Bauman peered over his glasses to gaze at his patient. "I assume there were animals you may have come in contact with?"

"Absolutely. Joseph, my brother-in-law, insisted the kids experience the life of a rancher, and even though I preferred a nice glass of Jack Daniels while sitting on the porch, I finally relented and joined them."

"What animals?"

"Cattle, buffalo, pigs, even crocodiles." Dominic smirked. "In the Northern Territory of Australia, they have crocs which we hunted, killed, and skinned."

"Oh my. I've never known you to embellish or carry on, Dominic. Not the type. I must say, I'm having a difficult time figuring out what's wrong, something clearly is, though. Hate to admit it, but I'm out of my league here. Too bad Marchetti is CEO now—best diagnostician I ever met, sent several of my puzzling cases to him to sort out over the past few years. I understand that even with his new duties, he insisted on leaving one afternoon free to see select patients. I'll try to capture a slot for you."

Dr. Dante Marchetti. The same man I'm choosing to squeeze. How fucked up would that be? Let me hold off for the time being. He seemed less than ecstatic tending to me at first.

CHAPTER SIXTY-ONE

Barry Isaacson, the hospital's newly appointed CFO, strutted briskly to the CEO's office. He rarely got summoned to his boss's office as of late and wondered what issue he wished to discuss. The fallout from the ransomware attack? The profit/loss numbers which had just come in? He wasn't certain, but he came prepared to address either.

"Come in, Barry. Barry, what's the amount of money left on the Federal loan for this new building?"

"100 million dollars, more or less."

"And the name of the consultant company they hired to make certain that our hospital stays solvent in order to pay back the loan?"

"Bellecon."

"When is their first visit with me scheduled?"

"We postponed it while this cyber security issue was playing out."

"I want the first meeting sooner than later. Okay?"

"Yes, I'll get on it right away." Isaacson's head cocked to the side, not at all certain why the CEO would desire to move up such a meeting.

***

The Bellecon people arrived on the scene en masse, six in all. Seated around Dan's desk in a semi-circle, each member took a minute or so to introduce themselves and their areas of expertise. Then their lead consultant, John Sorvino, began the session.

"Your hospital's presently losing a million dollars per quarter, and unless something is definitively done to wrangle significant cash, you run a serious risk of defaulting on your debt. The federal government that lent you the money ten years ago to build this facility can't allow that to happen," Sorvino lectured Marchetti, his blue and white striped tie with white button-down fitted shirt and blue suit a perfect combination for a man in his line of work. "You sure inherited a real economic disaster, Dr. Marchetti, when you were tapped for the CEO position."

Dan smirked.

"I believe as I look over your cost-cutting proposals that there exist some additional names of salaried specialists whose contracts should be terminated. Just need a little more time for me to perform my due diligence." Straight shooters with impeccable integrity and professionalism who couldn't be corrupted, Dan surmised. In contrast to several male and some female physicians he knew of or at least suspected were going to partner or already have done so with Antonetti's underworld friends.

"But surely, Mr. Sorvino, you'd agree that we can't solely cut our way to solvency?"

"This is true."

"Then our Emergency Room is our great feeder of patients for admissions: surgical, medical, and pediatrics. We need to apportion some money to expand its size, as all our analyses indicate that should we increase our volume in the Emergency Room by twenty percent, it would put us in the black."

"You're certain that the proposed increase in numbers would definitely be there should we ever secure the funds to enlarge the space?"

"Absolutely. Our data shows that at least twenty to fifty patients leave each day without being seen rather than wait outside, in the hallway, or in their cars."

"Can you furnish me those numbers, please?"

Dan didn't hesitate to hand him that packet, having anticipated the request.

"Will get back to you on this. I assume the projected costs and architectural workup's here as well?"

Dan nodded. "As you can see, I've done my homework." Though Bellecon's construction partners, Lombardi and Sons, Inc., would score the rigged bid when it went out. Better than no expansion, Dan reasoned.

"Dr. Marchetti, I want you to know that we don't hold you responsible at all for the plight this facility presently finds itself in. As a CEO who's only two months on the job, you could never be blamed for the fiscal shitstorm, pardon my street talk, that this place finds itself in."

"Thank you. But I own it now, for better or worse. Please get back to me soon."

"I will. We don't gain anything by wasting valuable time."

Dan concurred, acutely aware that time was of the essence in turning his hospital's finances around.

CHAPTER SIXTY-TWO

The crew leaned on their shovels, awaiting the backhoe to perform the heavy digging, the preparations for the expansion of the Emergency Room having been fast-tracked by the Federal government. A clear result of local politicians cashing in the chits owed them. That was how politics functioned, especially in Antonetti's world, and to say that Dr. Dante Marchetti was ecstatic with the decision-making would be a gross understatement.

In fact, Dan had decided to spend his lunch hour in a short-sleeved shirt, tie loosened and a Diet Coke in his hand, observing the excavation through his dark Ray-Ban sunglasses, a gift from the support staff in his office for his birthday. They thought they made him look distinguished. Dan stared at the soil being dug up.

"You appear to be looking for something, sir," remarked one of the more rotund workers, whose belly protruded many inches over the black back brace that all the men engaged in this physical labor were ordered to wear.

"You never know, you never know. Buried treasure," he joked. The words of the chief architect for the hospital still resonated in his mind. Dan gazed at his wristwatch and realized he needed to dash for his one o'clock meeting with the head of Radiology. Making his way to the entrance of the present Emergency Room, he recalled Higgins' words.

"The Board took many, many months arguing where the front of the hospital would reside so as not to dig up the bodies buried there." Undoubtedly from mafia-ordered hits. About to negotiate the one flight of stairs to his office, he overheard the unmistakable shouting of the backhoe operator, "Shit, I hit something firm, looks like a metal suitcase or something." Pointing directly in front of the backhoe he was maneuvering that afternoon, he watched as the member of the excavation team who'd previously attempted to manufacture small talk with the CEO bent over ever so slowly to grab the handle of the large object, a piece of luggage indeed. The exertion needed to lift its considerable weight caused him to breathe ever so rapidly.

"Holy shit, maybe there's money in it. Open it up!" Yelled one younger member of the team, his eyes wide in anticipation.

"It's got a lock, grab the metal cutters." Once handed the tool, he dispatched the lock quickly and hurriedly opened the surprise find. As soon as it was open, the men were overcome with one of the most horrific, nauseating smells they'd ever experienced, including those of the dead animals they occasionally came across. Inside, enclosed in clear, plastic tarp was the disintegrating remains of a dead human being, minus hands, feet, and head.

Two of the men turned their back to the find and threw up their breakfasts while others covered their noses with the ends of their work shirts.

Bingo, the architect told the truth. Now to turn this discovery into something valuable.

***

The opened suitcase lay on a stainless-steel table, one of its hinges now dangling because of its rough handling and the weight of overlying earth. Before the FBI transferred the item to its forensic lab, it did its usual thorough analysis of the crime scene, which meant that everything was painstakingly documented—from the presence of shell casings (none found) or other artifacts which may have evidentiary value, down to the color and texture of the underlying soil. This forensic anthropology method was based on years of archaeological science, concepts, and methods to recover not only the evidence and the remains, but also the information and the context of what was in those burials.

Finally, the remains were ready to be examined, grisly work to be sure and only fitting for a particular subset of individuals, namely the forensic scientist. They routinely confined their search to the "big four"—identifying age, sex, race, and stature.

They were armed with the knowledge that a corpse generally progresses through five stages of decomposition—fresh, bloat (autolysis), active decay (putrefaction), advanced decay, and skeletonization.

The brain was one of the first parts of the body to break down. A few minutes after death, its cells collapse and release water. Then other energy-guzzling organs follow. Microbes then eat through the gut and escape into the rest of the body.

The forensic scientist reported that the smell in this case, which was especially putrid, invariably indicated that death occurred four to ten days prior when autolysis took place and gases and discoloration started. Direct analysis of certain genomic sequences present in the white blood cells proved invaluable for DNA and it was much less susceptible to degradation than proteins, enzymes, and antigens. RFLP DNA testing was statistically individualizing (one out of several million or several billion) and had withstood rigorous court challenges on its validity. This method also usually required a large sample size to obtain significant results, which was present in the hospital case.

***

"Arturo Christopher Pugliano, who the fuck is that?" That was the name that matched the DNA retrieved from the excavation site abutting the hospital. Male, forty-six years old, 5'4" in height and about 195 pounds, Italian, and of stocky build. Incidentally, four healed rib fractures were noted and a retained bullet in the upper right thigh.

"Smalltime hood with a long rap sheet and ties to the Mafucci family. Fractured trachea, most likely from a strangulation. Buried by an individual probably not aware of the upcoming Emergency Room expansion. The head was found elsewhere during the excavation inside an oversized foam rubber glove of the sort one could buy at a sporting event." The joke around the coroner's office was that the head fit the torso "like a glove."

What the find did accomplish was to put a significant halt to the construction project to expand the Emergency Room, as the police officials determined that this area was more than likely a burial ground for more corpses that needed to be disposed of quickly and efficiently. "No wonder the Board was so split on the ER expansion, when every reasonable hospital official knew that the present facility was crying out for more space," Dan pondered out loud.

CHAPTER SIXTY-THREE

Dominic couldn't remember feeling so poorly for so long before. The past month had been a shitshow, losing twenty pounds, getting so damn weak and short of breath that he slept downstairs in a guest room to avoid the stairs.

I'm fuckin' dying here. I'm only fifty-four, Goddammit!

"Dr. Bauman, please get me an appointment with Dr. Marchetti. I can't go on like this anymore."

"No problem, Dominic. Smart decision. He's that good." With that, the older, soon to be retired physician called Marchetti's office and because of their longstanding relationship, was put right through to the new CEO.

"Dan, Michael. How are things in the C-suite these days?" Bauman asked.

"Putting out fires right and left, up and down," Dan answered half-jokingly, maybe not even half.

"Heavy is the head that wears the crown, as they say."

"What can I do for you old friend?" Dan changed the subject.

If he only knew that half of it.

"Would like you to see a patient for me as a second opinion, damnedest case."

"For you, of course. What gives?"

"Fifty-four-year-old male, recently returned from a month-long vacation on a working farm in Australia, presented with frequent episodes of diarrhea, weakness, shortness of breath, and so on. A metabolic acidosis and a whole host of other abnormal values… Anyway, his records will be in his electronic medical record in our system along with my summary to date."

"Okay, what's his name?" Dan had taken a pen to write the information down.

"Dominic Antonetti."

Dan froze, the pen dropping from his hand.

"Dominic Antonetti?"

"That's correct. He's requesting you."

How ironic, trying to utilize the same healthcare institution and medical capabilities that he's simultaneously attempting to steal tens of millions from. Chutzpah of the highest order!

***

Dan finished changing into his lab coat while checking his watch. He had a tight schedule and very mixed feelings about seeing his first patient that morning, Dominic Antonetti. Hippocratic Oath or not, where did it say that a physician must see a patient who's unscrupulous and trying to rob the very institution he seeks help from in a time of need? Dan recalled a surgeon during his training who relayed a story of a young boy who'd been run over by a car and sustained numerous internal injuries, including a ruptured spleen and damaged liver. He operated on the poor kid successfully, essentially saving his young life, though he did sustain permanent orthopedic disabilities. Imagine the shock he experienced when he was later sued as part of an all-encompassing malpractice suit naming every physician involved in the care of this unfortunate child! Astonishingly, six months later the father required his gallbladder to be removed and, lo and behold, requested that same general surgeon to perform the surgery. He demurred.

Marchetti, no different than many other providers, decided to take on this challenging case despite his reservations. He'd focus on the clinical puzzle itself and not the nature of the patient's character.

When Dan entered his examination room, he was struck by the aging process that had overtaken his patient. His hair no longer appeared as full, his skin, instead of an olive hue, was sallow, while his shirt hung on his abdomen instead of exhibiting his usual paunch. He had the kind of weight loss that never looked complimentary but that of an intensely diminished individual.

"Mr. Antonetti. I understand we've not been feeling well as of late." No reason to exchange the usual greetings, as both men knew the score.

After peppering his patient with a long list of standard medical questions, Dan switched gears and focused his attention on travel history, to which Antonetti described his family's vacationing in Australia at a relative's farm. While not making his usual direct and foreboding eye contact, Dominic Antonetti peered directly at his hands and spoke, his voice thin and raspy.

"Dr. Marchetti, I had some exposure to cattle, buffalo, pigs, and, yes, crocodiles. In addition, I helped spray pesticides—the full farming experience with my family—and stupidly, I chose not to wear gloves or protective clothing despite being told to do so by my brother-in-law."

"Why not?" Dan inquired.

"It was too damn hot!" He answered defensively, but quickly regained his composure. "I went barefoot oftentimes when not working. Oh, almost forgot, I drank from freshwater dams when hiking with the family."

Dan realized then that Antonetti couldn't have exposed himself to more dangerous pathogens if he'd tried.

Methodically entering all this information, plus the answers to many other inquiries that took over forty minutes, his mind reverted once again to the clinical possibilities. Once he examined his patient, he was taken aback by his low blood pressure and the acetone odor on his breath.

"I want you to go to the lab and have more blood taken for a number of additional tests," Dan instructed his patient before exiting the room.

"Can you tell me what you're thinking, Doctor?" Antonetti sounded unusually obsequious at that moment. This physician held his very life in his hands. No more John Gotti bravado.

"Still too early, but I have some thoughts, especially related to your exposure histories. Though those exposures may constitute a red herring."

"A red herring, you say. Sorry, I don't get it."

"Oh, clues or information that can mislead or distract from the truth."

"I see." Dominic hesitated, his brown eyes moistening. "I'm grateful and put all my trust in you."

Dan grimaced at the hypocrisy when his back was turned and exited the room quickly without acknowledging his patient's thankfulness.

CHAPTER SIXTY-FOUR

Dominic anxiously listened for the sound of hard-soled shoes in the hallway, which would indicate that Dr. Marchetti was about to pay him the promised visit made on the phone earlier. After waiting two and a half hours since his hospital bed opened up, the object of his anticipation strolled purposefully into his room.

"Mr. Antonetti, I've put you in the hospital because I'm convinced you have a serious systemic illness, and we can no longer justify continuing the workup as an outpatient."

"I understand," responded Antonetti shakily, trying to sound unperturbed but failing miserably.

He was fuckin' scared.

"Please tell me what you know, Doc, I'm a big boy."

"Okay. Your blood pressure is a bit low, though your lungs sound fine and your belly exam's normal."

"I'm following you so far. I think. I may not look it, but I have a decent head on my shoulders," he offered.

Trying to level the playing ground.

"I'm sure you do," Dan responded while glancing at his patient.

Clever like a fox, unfortunately.

"These skin lesions and pigmented areas on your arms and legs. How long have they been there?"

"Not certain. Thought they were just age spots, no?"

"Maybe. Okay. Your kidney function's a bit off, the sodium and potassium in your blood are low, and several other tests are abnormal. But you're not diabetic. It's my job to put this all together and I will. Have a little patience, alright?"

There was no mistaking the seriousness in his voice nor his resolve in diagnosing this condition. After all, Dan didn't earn the moniker 'doctor's doctor' for no reason.

"Less likely was that you sustained a pesticide or herbicide toxicity, which if I did believe it strongly would require in some cases an immediate antidote treatment and supportive care. Poisoning with a heavy metal's still possible, but an infectious cause for all of this is still very high on my list. I'm going to start you on antibiotics just in case and before my testing comes back, to get ahead of it."

"What infections? I can look them up on WebMD." Dominic took out a notebook to record. Dan always appreciated when patients took an interest like this. Most of the time, it could prove helpful, although in some instances, frankly speaking, a real pain in the ass.

"L-e-p-t-o-s-p-i-r-o-s-i-s, Q Fever, r-i-c-k-e-t-t-s-i-a-l infections, and m-e-l-i-o-i-d-o-s-i-s."

"Got it. Thank you. I appreciate what you're doing." Dominic looked away when he uttered those words.

What have I done yet? Dan thought. *Nothing much.*

***

Day three of his hospitalization saw Dominic Antonetti's diarrhea stop, while CAT scans of his head, chest, abdomen, and pelvis showed some fluid in the spaces about his lungs and in his abdominal cavity, but small amounts. No abscesses or pneumonias. The other numbers had normalized in the meantime with treatment.

While Dan sat at the computer, documenting all Antonetti's progress, including his latest values and tests, his primary nurse approached him. "Dr. Marchetti, our patient has just become quite agitated, and visually hallucinating." Marchetti rose from his chair to quickly assess the situation.

"Dominic, where are you now?"

"I… I don't know. Home?"

"No, you're in the hospital, and we're treating your illness."

"My illness? What illness? Besides, don't you hate me?"

"I don't hate you Dominic," Dan lied.

Why? Just because you're trying to bankrupt this hospital and cripple my stewardship of the very same institution that's trying to save your life? Nonsense.

Addressing the nurse now, sidestepping the question, he said, "Need to schedule an MRI and I'll need to tap his CSF. Let me go back and write the orders as well as prescribe something to calm him down." With that, the new CEO and highly conflicted physician went about his business. It was a diagnostic dilemma, for certain. Who knew what he would find now?

***

"Now that hurt like hell, Doc." Dominic Antonetti complained to the hematologist after he completed retrieving the bone marrow from his patient.

"Apologies. Very difficult to deaden the marrow with an anesthetic agent, I'm sorry to say. All done, though." Dan had observed the procedure and marched the material down to pathology himself. Once there, he handed over the specimens to the tech directly, ensuring no lost sample could occur, which in a hospital of their size, happened not too infrequently.

"Please prepare the slides stat, Walter, I need to know the results as soon as possible."

"Will do."

True to his word, later that day Dan received a call from the lab tech, known throughout the facility as extremely efficient and highly professional.

"*Dyserythropoiesis*"—abnormal red blood cells— "Sir, but white cells look normal in shape. Most likely from a toxin, a drug, or simply severe illness alone."

"You're certain?" Dan asked needlessly, for he knew Walter would doublecheck his work always and if in doubt, would tell him so.

"You bet."

"Thanks, appreciate it."

What's going on with you, Mr. Dominic Antonetti? It's high time for you to shed some additional light on this whole matter if possible.

CHAPTER SIXTY-FIVE

Dan finished his extremely busy day while also considering all the possibilities that would explain Antonetti's symptoms: so-called "zoonotic" infections emanating from farm animals, infections derived from organisms in the soil, or some unknown toxin at that point circulating in his sickened body.

Leptospirosis, the first bacteria that came to mind, could've been transmitted from the urine of infected animals, oftentimes deposited in swimming holes, or if he might've come in contact with a pig carcass during the slaughtering process. That would explain the numerous diarrheal bouts and protracted vomiting.

Melioidosis, another organism that contaminated the soil in the Northern Territory of Australia could enter through the skin. His patient had rambled barefoot at times, could have breathed the organism in, or ingested it with food.

Additionally, certain pesticides could be readily absorbed through the skin and could produce some of his patient's symptoms, while specific herbicides could produce some of the additional lab abnormalities that he possessed. Dan's gut said this was very unlikely, though.

Thallium and even arsenic could cause these symptoms but then again, why these agents? He was tired, his thought process craving some dinner; it was time to get on home. Lauren was coming over with some pasta dish and frankly, he missed her company and her laughter.

***

Dan stared at the MRI, about which he now remained in agreement with the always jovial raconteur, Dr. Myron Levy of the Radiology Department. Myron's jokes were funny even though he tended to take the scenic route when telling them.

"Unremarkable." Additionally, the results of the spinal tap he performed were also entirely normal.

"What the fuck?" He muttered out loud, assured that nobody was around to hear the new CEO curse. "At least he seems to be improving.

Kidney function's now normal, antibiotics have been discontinued." Dan liked to talk out loud; his mother did the same thing. How often when she went to the mudroom to wash the family's clothes did he or his brother hear their mother engage in an imaginary conversation with herself? Now it was his turn.

Genetics tell the story.

***

The next day told a completely different tale. Liver function tests were abruptly getting worse, a hepatitis progression, and all three blood cell lines, white cells, red cells, and platelets were low. Dominic Antonetti's bone marrow was severely depressed and producing only a fraction of the cells needed to sustain life. These findings opened a whole new can of worms. It was not lost on Dan that he was pulling on a ball of twine that seemed to have no end in sight!

11.00 PM and Marchetti sat up in bed contemplating his patient's latest findings. Picking up his cellphone, despite the late hour, he dialed his superb Chair of Medicine who he appointed to replace himself when he received his promotion. Dr. Valentin Albescu, born in Romania, had been an earlier resident in training, a brilliant young physician whose fund of knowledge was so superior that he routinely scored in the 99th percentile on standardized medical knowledge exams with his only shortcoming at the time his command of the English language.

"Valentin, sorry to bother you, dear friend. Got a clinical conundrum for you."

"No problem, sir. Those are the best kind."

Dan recounted his patient's entire case to date, taking care not to leave any detail out. "Been thinking that HLH should be considered, Valentin—your thoughts?"

"Multisystem involvement, to be sure, reduced cell lines but no fever makes it less likely."

"Low platelets or bone marrow abnormality as well."

"No destruction of red blood cells though. Antibiotic-induced toxicity?"

"Maybe," countered Dan, "but my gut says no. Going to order another bone marrow aspiration and biopsy for tomorrow."

"Absolutely."

"You know, Valentin, I'm so tired, I'm going to call it a night. If any other idea comes to mind, you know where to reach me. Thanks for taking my call."

"Nonsense. I'm honored that you would even consider asking for my opinion. You taught me everything, Dr. Marchetti."

"Flattering, but entirely not true. Goodnight."

Tomorrow should bring me closer to the answer.

CHAPTER SIXTY-SIX

Finally, the verdict came in, forestalling the painful procedures planned for that day. *Arsenic poisoning*, according to the lab. But how? When confirming that Dominic Antonetti hadn't eaten any seafood days before falling ill, the test for heavy metals came back, evidencing an arsenic level of 5100 micrograms per liter in his urine and 326 micrograms per liter in his blood. Normally a patient should register no more than fifty-two micrograms in either urine or blood.

When Dan entered Antonetti's room that Monday morning, he encountered a nurse opening a milk container for him while inserting a straw from her patient's food tray. Marchetti sat in a chair in the corner of the room, a few feet from Antonetti's hospital bed. After exchanging a quick greeting, the physician waited until the nurse exited. The truth was that he wished to relay his findings to the man alone, especially because of its possible implications.

"Dominic, I have the answer as to why you're so sick," Dan said, moving to the edge of the bed to face his gangster patient.

"Oh?" Dominic blurted out, his thin, haggard face—once considered ruggedly attractive—registering a mixture of anticipation and abject fear at the words to follow.

"Arsenic poisoning, and at very high levels, I'm afraid."

"Arsenic poisoning? Arsenic poisoning, you say?" He remained frozen for a good ten seconds, his enfeebled mind trying to construct a rationale for it all. "Can it be treated?"

"Yes, it can. The treatment involves a process called chelation, whereby we give you a medicine called succimer. It comes in a pill form at a prescribed schedule for almost three weeks. Now, it's possible you sustained these levels by drinking the fresh dam water in Australia, known for containing high levels of this metal."

"Didn't drink but a cupped handful, Doctor." Dominic squinted and exhibited the body language of the hunter instead of the cowering prey. No, this dangerous substance made its way into his body by the nefarious actions of one of his many enemies. Several culprits came to mind, for a man in his position possessed no shortage of individuals wishing to do him harm. "I was poisoned, Doctor. I'll bet what is left of this tawdry life on it."

CHAPTER SIXTY-SEVEN

"How're you feeling today?" Marchetti inquired, sitting at Antonetti's bedside that Sunday morning, holding his cup of Starbucks in one hand.

"I have a new symptom this morning, Doctor," Dominic said, bursting into tears, the entire ordeal threatening to break the spirit of a man who once believed himself a so-called "Rock of Gibraltar."

Strangely, Dan felt tremendous sorrow at the sight of this man to whom a new malady seemed to occur on a regular basis.

"What is it, Dominic?" Dan put his drink down on the windowsill, patting the sick man's hand to comfort him. Compassion for an ailing human being was never far from Marchetti's inner soul, despite what heinous acts the morally corrupt man had committed. Strange circumstances, to say the least.

"There's a tingling sensation in my hands and feet and a vibrating feeling in my feet also. And…" He sobbed openly now with no attempt to hide his despair, "When I wandered into the bathroom, I couldn't actually feel my feet on the floor." Dominic reached for a tissue, "I'm dying, aren't I, Dr. Marchetti?"

The hairs on Dan's neck all stood on end.

The last time a patient made such a statement was an elderly black woman with an overactive thyroid. Because of her impoverished state, other institutions had dragged their feet in treating her. She asked just that question, only to pass from a malignant arrythmia that very night, despite Marchetti reassuring her to the contrary.

After putting his patient through various targeted maneuvers, he concluded that his patient now exhibited a polyneuropathy, or damage to the long nerves that convey sensation to the brain. Dominic Antonetti's arsenic poisoning had damaged his peripheral nerves.

***

Weeks later, once again reclaiming his equilibrium after the treatment proved beneficial, Dominic reminded himself that there was the matter of thanking Dr. Marchetti for essentially giving him back his life. He could have recused himself from helping a man who'd severely sabotaged his herculean efforts to save the Sacred Heart Hospital. Point of fact, dealing with his newfound sense of dismay, of utter disgust rather, at having "bitten the hand that saved him," so to speak, threatened to cause his very being to convulse from deep-seeded guilt and shamefulness. Furthermore, considering himself a practicing Catholic, how could he ever enter God's Kingdom with a resume like he owned? How could a devout Catholic, or perhaps not so devout, make it right with his Lord?

CHAPTER SIXTY-EIGHT

Scott loved the nighttime, its peacefulness, its serenity. Just the atmosphere where the desire to get high would serve as an invisible magnet for him to reach for something, anything to help him get stoned. In practice, it was the best time for an active SEAL to perform all their clandestine activities. Though those days seemed so far away, the principle still applied. He imagined every conceivable scenario and what steps he'd need to take to ensure success with the plan he was about to carry out. He recalled the time he'd emerged from a nighttime mission in Afghanistan totally covered in his victims' blood, with the choice of weapons in that instance ranging from customized carbines to primitive tomahawks. Yes, tomahawks, which some eschewed due to their bulkiness, but he found the weapon's utility in certain kill situations such as close hand-to-hand combat. Other times he cruised on boats which were really spying stations, or as a civilian working in a travel agency.

The truth was that the Navy's SEAL Team Six, of which he was once a proud member was secretive, scantily scrutinized, and a myth to most Americans.

Scott himself had become an integral member of the Omega Program; an initiative assigned to the SEALs who'd joined forces with handpicked CIA operatives. They enjoyed essentially no oversight. The cost was steep, as more members had perished in the past decade and a half since he'd joined than in all its previous history. Scott himself had suffered no less than twelve separate fractured bones from repeated kill missions, parachute jumps, climbs up impossible mountain terrains, and more explosive blasts than he cared to remember. The injuries had led him down that slippery path to reliance on narcotics for pain relief. How ironic—a job that provided him tremendous self-worth at a time he so craved it, but also an addiction that had forced him into a downward, perilous spiral.

The bottom line, however, was that they were trained to thrive in extremely complex and swift-moving environments. At times, their tasks would be considered grisly to those outside the team, as they needed to cut off fingers or patches of scalp for DNA analysis from freshly killed militants. The years of nightly raids had helped to unravel Taliban networks. Furthermore, at times they utilized customized German-made rifles with suppressors which uniformly reduced sounds and muzzle flashes, while their infrared lasers enabled the SEALs to shoot more accurately at night. Along with thermal optics to detect body heat, their equipment provided them distinct advantages over their enemies. Grenades of the thermobaric kind were used when needing to ensure that a building would collapse so few enemies were able to escape alive.

The name itself, SEAL, was an acronym that stood for Sea, Air, Land forces. The even-numbered groups like his trained in Virginia Beach, the odd-numbered in San Diego, while a separate unit altogether dedicated to mini-submarines trained in beautiful Hawaii. Suffice to say, the training itself was so severe that half of all participants washed out before completing their tasks, no matter the location.

SEAL team members were taught to "slice and dice every major artery."

Most importantly, if ever one were to feel even slightly threatened, then "you're going to kill somebody."

Mistakes were unfortunately committed. There was that highly tragic instance when eight local Afghan high school students were executed for being misidentified and essentially being in the wrong place at the wrong time. What made the SEALs particularly deadly was their uncanny ability and refined techniques that enabled them to sneak up on enemy compounds. Of note was the time Scott and his group sky-dived into Somalia using a freefall parachuting technique called "HAHO," in which they'd jumped from a high altitude so they could steer their way on the wind for many miles to cross a border secretly, an exercise so risky that Scott personally saw fatalities while training. Team Six approached in the dark and instantly killed all nine captors while rescuing the two captive American aide workers unharmed and without incurring any injury or fatality themselves.

Towards the end of his service, Scott participated with a female member of the elite group, admitted by the Navy to a unit called the Black Squadron. The idea was simple: that working in a male and female pair facilitated "profile softening" or making the couple appear less suspicious to hostile militant groups or intelligence services. Her name had been Felicia, and he'd fell in love with her almost instantly because of her irresistible combination of striking midwestern good looks, brilliant mind, and tough-as-nails personality. She had been captured, tortured, and dismembered on her maiden mission. Scott had been devastated but made sure that the individuals that committed such a barbaric act prayed to die quickly after he and his team caught up with them.

Members of this Russian mafia responsible for his sister's poisoning and orchestrating his newly identified father's misery could expect no less from him.

CHAPTER SIXTY-NINE

Dominic Antonetti tried to go about his business as if the past seventy-two hours had never happened, though it proved to be much trickier than he'd believed. Having one's life saved by someone whose professional life you'd attempted to corrupt unmercifully was a game-changer. The previous night he finished reading *Preparing for Jesus' Return: Daily Live the Blessed Hope* by A. W. Tozer. He'd copied down a passage onto a three by five card, which he now impulsively retrieved from his trouser pocket to read once again the words:

If a man had his way, the plan of redemption would be an endless and bloody conflict. In reality, salvation was brought not by Jesus' fist, but by His nail-pierced hands; not by muscle but by love; not by vengeance but by forgiveness; not by force but by sacrifice.

"I must put an end to this madness," he said out loud. As he stirred the sugar in his coffee, he committed then and there to informing the Russian boss, Alexei Dobrynin, that despite their frustration at his being unsuccessful in turning the recalcitrant physician, Marchetti was better off alive than dead. Since Dominic Antonetti's business had proven quite profitable to his counterpart's organization, surely he remained safe, he reasoned, from any reprisals or retribution for not heeding this order. *Basta*, or at least he hoped so. However, the arsenic poisoning was a clear signal from one of his enemies, but from whom?

Purtroppo, ci sono molti.

There were so many.

***

Scott peered off into the distance while leaning against the hood of his 1986 Mustang with over 386,000 miles on the clock, just purchased for a relative pittance. To say his savings were meager would be an understatement, though his sister had gifted him some funds to help tide him over while he continued with his rehab.

Almost every ship entering the Port of New York and New Jersey from the Atlantic Ocean must first pass underneath the Verrazano–

Narrows Bridge, connecting Brooklyn, NY, with Staten Island. The sea and its large vessels had always fascinated him, and situating himself under this 684-foot-tall bridge provided quite a view.

Scott checked his equipment, which he'd been surprisingly allowed to keep after leaving the Navy. It had been irregular, but it helped having saved the life of someone in the armaments department. SEAL operators were trained on a variety of small arms and heavy weapons, including pistols, rifles, machine guns, sniper rifles, rocket and missile launchers, grenades, and explosives, but the most valuable weapons system is the operator. On many occasions, Scott attempted to sell these weapons of war for desperately needed money for drugs, only to fail miserably. It seemed that likely buyers believed the operation to represent some sting orchestrated by a homeland security official, not unusual at all. So, he managed to find a fortuitous hiding spot in an abandoned shed located on foreclosed property destined to remain that way.

Brighton Beach was a neighborhood in the southern portion of the Brooklyn borough of New York City, well-known for its abundant population of Russian-speaking immigrants and as a summer destination for New York City residents seeking the beaches along the Atlantic Ocean or the amusement parks in Coney Island. The years just before and following the Great Depression saw a large percentage of Jewish-Americans settle there. This was followed by a sizeable influx of Holocaust concentration camp survivors.

In the 1970s, Brighton Beach became a sought-after area for Soviet immigrants, mostly Ashkenazi Jews from Russia and Ukraine. The 1991 collapse of the Soviet Union led to thousands of additional Russian immigrants seeking refuge there. Russian stores opened throughout, with storefront signs containing both English and Russian names. along with luxury condominiums, "Oceana" for one, which was constructed in the early 2000s.

One of the older, larger private homes located just to the west of the Oceana building served as a meeting place for one particular Russian mob, and Scott had noted that such a gathering was taking place involving numerous *Shestyorka* (soldiers), a *Bratok* or associate of the Brigadier, a *Derzhatel Obshchaka*, the money collector, and the other Spy or security officer. Again, the former SEAL team member who was trained to operate in complex and difficult situations that were fast-moving knew exactly what weapon to employ. A thermobaric grenade, proficient in making an entire building collapse upon itself, would suffice nicely.

The lights from the luxury condominium lit up the area so efficiently that each individual owner and family member felt safe in coming and going at all hours of the night as many were apt to do, especially during the warmer months. Today would be no exception, July 4th. The noise generated from this grenade, though unusually loud, could conceivably be mistaken initially as powerful fireworks. Of course, the resultant building collapse would be noticed after a few moments, so Scott would most assuredly need to get in and out quickly.

He dressed in dark material with face paint and a dark woolen cap. Sidling up to the back door entrance would permit access into the kitchen area, where some kind of card game was entertaining all the men. Attaching a small amount of C-4 explosive material to open the door in case it was locked, he encountered a *Shestyorka* balancing himself against the wall of the building with one foot while he puffed on a Russian cigarette. He gazed at the ground contemplating something crucial, like when he was going to get laid next. Without any wasted movement at all, Scott crushed the man's windpipe with his fist, held him up while he planted the C-4, quickly detonated the device, kicked open the door, and activated the grenade, which he pressed against his now unconscious foot soldier. Shoving him viciously onto the card table, his last word was shouted loudly and joyfully, *"Privyet!"*

Diving back out through the entrance, Scott awaited the blast, which ensued immediately, and it wasn't until he'd travelled a dozen meters or more that he looked back to see the walls implode, the roof shattering while the first floor crashed to the basement level exactly on cue. A true house of cards. No one could've survived the blast and, sure enough, when he quickly returned to surveil the exploded site, all were extremely dead, a mass of body parts with one head still demonstrating a lit *Belomorkanal* in his mouth.

***

Today the Brigadier—the *Avtoritet* ("Authority") who functioned like a captain in charge of a small group of men, like a Caporegime in the Italian American mafia, responsible for giving out jobs to his warriors and paying substantial tribute to the boss—today, he'd retire permanently from his roles. Scott's specially equipped German-made rifle with its suppressor addition and state-of-the-art infrared laser would ensure just that.

The moonless night was ideal and the Russian nightclub in Brighton Beach the location, frequented every Tuesday night like clockwork by his target. Situated comfortably in the back seat of his van, Scott's window was slightly rolled down, enough to identify his mark rather handily. The sidewalk in front of the club was poorly lit, despite its need to advertise its business. Maybe they didn't want to attract any outsiders.

Thirty-two minutes later, to be exact, the Brigadier arrived on foot with his small entourage, right on time, stopping to put out his cigarette on the bottom of his shoe. When opportunity knocks... The top of his skull exploded like an overripe watermelon, with each of his companions now splattered with bone, soft tissue, brain matter, and of course, blood. Scott calmly hoisted himself into his driver's seat and left the premises swiftly and quietly, having allowed his vehicle to idle the whole time so as not to alert attention by starting his engine. In and out seamlessly, a SEAL Team specialty.

CHAPTER SEVENTY

Scott Mason found it quite simple to evade the security system that the boss employed in his resplendent waterfront estate, right there in the heart of his place of business, Brighton Beach. Overcoming the two bodyguards patrolling outside proved to be straightforward for this special forces veteran. Both men were left exsanguinating, one from a transected right carotid artery and the other a macerated femoral artery, tomahawked so severely that his limb hung by a tendinous remnant and fractured left femur bone.

The head of this Russian mob would meet a different conclusion to his miserable life. An eye for an eye. It was the *Pakhan's* decision to attempt to kill by poisoning his beloved sister Lauren, so it'd be a reversal of sorts that he'd engineer for him. Approaching his target, who was soundly asleep in his garishly decorated bedroom without registering any appreciable disturbance, again a SEAL team specialty, Scott held his handgun firmly against the boss's right temple while his right hand covered his prey's now wide-open mouth and malevolent eyes. The cloth was soaked in strychnine, a highly toxic, bitter-tasting neurotoxin which primarily affects the motor nerve fibers in the spinal cord, finally causing severe muscular contractions, not of the normal kind but spastic ones resulting in an excruciatingly frightening state of asphyxiation. It was puzzling to think that in the early 1900s this lethal substance was used as a performance enhancer. One notorious use was during the 1904 Olympics Marathon, when the track-and-field athlete Thomas Hicks, against his wishes, had been administered a mixture of egg whites and brandy laced with a minuscule amount of strychnine to "elevate his stamina." He had finished the race victoriously, though he'd completed it actively hallucinating before collapsing.

"I could've injected you, which would've killed you in very short order, but a bastard like you doesn't deserve such a humane act. This way I get to watch the process where you realize that in just a few minutes you'll suffer so outrageously that the only thing that will cross your tortured mind will be how to get one last breath into those cigarette-stained lungs of yours."

"*Babla,*" he muttered under his breath, sitting up in bed while Scott nestled into a soft chair a few feet from him, gun aimed directly at his head, the suppressor clearly visible. "My men, what... What did you do to them?"

"Oh well. You know their spilled blood, of which there was plenty, is probably clotted by now. Probably looks like borsch. You like borsch?"

The boss propelled himself towards his captor but landed awkwardly and short of his target on the wooden floor, the audible crack of a few ribs the only sound heard. All at once the strychnine began to block all the acetylcholine receptors, the victim's chest resting on the hardwood floor while his rigid body was positioned like he completed a freefall skydive. Both arms extended above the floor, legs spreadeagled with toes forming a bridge with the floor beneath him. The boss's eyes bulged forward. Asphyxia was a horrendous way to die and the dying mobster, king of Brighton Beach, turned a deep bluish hue due to a lack of oxygen. At that point, Scott experienced a change of heart and placed a bullet neatly in the middle of his forehead.

CHAPTER SEVENTY-ONE

Sasha Makedonsky woke very early, as was his custom when the day's activities centered around murdering someone. It was another chance to prove his mettle to the boss after having fled Mother Russia, narrowly escaping a lifetime prison sentence in their draconian penal system. Found guilty of rape, he'd managed to jump out of the courtroom window and miraculously escape in a hearse driven by his brother-in-law, waiting for him outside with the motor running. They'd left the scene immediately before anyone could react. Forced to leave Russia for Athens, he'd finally ended up in Brighton Beach.

Soon after, Sasha joined the Russian mafia and was assigned the job of killing a man who'd enjoyed a one-night stand with the Brigadier's Ukrainian mistress. He'd strangled the man to death after dousing him with acid and dismembering the mistress while still alive.

Killing hadn't always been his line of work, as he'd been a graduate of a music school and worked for a space industry factory in Moscow. Soon thereafter he'd been drafted into the Russian army and assigned to their elite marine corps. That was where the taste of terminating another human being's life was awakened in his DNA.

Now he'd been assigned a much more strategic hit, a business associate whose conscience had suddenly reared its ugly head. No matter, Sasha possessed what his peers described as "superhuman marksmanship" qualities. Furthermore, for the best, only the deadliest of weapons was given to him by his employer—the top dog sniper rifle, the AI AXSR. No more misfires with the old Soviet-era SVD which had been around for more than a half-century. He loved its engineering, which gave it an unparalleled mixture of toughness, innovation, and incredible accuracy out to 2,000 meters and beyond. Sasha in fact told his boss that the rifle's capabilities were nothing short of jaw-dropping up to a target 2,200 meters away.

This poor fool won't know what hit him.
***

Sasha learned about the murders of the Pakhan, the Brigadier, and the two Shestyorkas in short order. The outrage he felt was indescribable and he favored a violent retaliation to be visited upon whomever was responsible for such a brazen affront to their beloved organization. Loyalty was another strong suit.

But who would lead this Brighton Beach group now? Furthermore, didn't he merit consideration, having forsaken a family and abided diligently with all eighteen code stipulations, however outdated? No modest task in this day and age. Besides, his exploits were how legends were made, weren't they? Piling up successful kills, the numbers too great to count anymore, not just in figures but sheer brutality.

Breaking his concentration was Valeri Petrov, a dangerous man in his own right, sidling up beside him at the neighborhood speakeasy, his toothy smile his characteristic trademark. He had so many gold-filled teeth that his mouth exhibited very few unaffected ones, a strange look. Nevertheless, people feared him in Brighton Beach, which suited him fine, except for maybe Sasha, his competition for the title of boss.

"You heard, my friend, of this massacre. Who's responsible?"

"Not certain. *Zashkvar.*" Disgraceful, he called it, acting as if men in his line of work never committed such acts. We seldom see ourselves for what we are.

The assassin or assassins better pray hard, day and night, not for a bright future but for a merciful death.

CHAPTER SEVENTY-TWO

Fall, 1999

Dan took a quick glance at his watch. 2:30 in the morning and he had morning report at seven AM sharp. Ballete didn't tolerate late arrivals at morning report unless the absence was patient-related; the venerable Chairman of Medicine was old-school all the way.

Dan had ordered three colorful kites from a well-known company and was busy assembling them according to the easy-to-follow directions. The twins would undoubtedly get a real kick out of the whole experience, and it would add some spice to their day together over the coming Sunday. A much-needed day off from his arduous 100-hour work week.

That Sunday, Dan waited anxiously for a response to the doorbell, beaming with excitement as he always did when spending the day with his children. Ever since their mother had made the difficult decision to allow Dan to participate in their young lives, he truly felt that they were a gift from God. Though true that he'd been merely a donor of semen, the relationship had become more than that. Surprisingly, the would-be single mother had acquiesced to allowing him to be a part of their lives.

"Good morning, Dan. The twins are devouring their breakfasts. What've you got here?" The twins' mother motioned towards the shopping bag full of kite paraphernalia.

"Thought the kids would enjoy watching some kites soar into the sky?" He replied, his eyes sparkling with joy.

"They'll love it. Thank you, Dan, for caring."

Hearing his voice from the kitchen, the children came hurrying to greet him. Dan looked back at their mother, who appeared completely fatigued. She'd developed a postpartum cardiomyopathy soon after giving birth and her heart had been weakened severely. Though some women recovered totally from this condition, many did not and eventually required a heart transplant after medicines fail to ameliorate the symptoms of heart failure.

"How're you feeling? You look worn out."

A nervous laugh ensued. "I'm afraid I'll need to go on that transplant list after all," she blurted out, trying desperately to not cry in front of the children.

"I'll talk with your cardiologist." He never got a chance—she died from an arrythmia the next day. After her passing, their aunt, Geri Marchand, found herself thrust into a newfound caretaker role as next of kin, initially flustered and ill prepared, but slowly warming to the task.

CHAPTER SEVENTY-THREE

Dominic Antonetti was in the process of finishing up a phone call but had notified his driver to meet him out in front of his office building. Salvatore had done just about anything for his boss over the sixteen years he'd worked for him, many unsavory. Though for now, driving occupied most of his present-day functions. Morbidly obese, he had trouble getting around, and add to that his ravaged lungs from years of smoking and bad hips, this new role suited him fine. Lighting up a cigarette while he waited, Big Sal pushed the button to open the window, since his boss loathed a car reeking from that "wretched tobacco smell." Sticking his huge head out the window while exhaling from deep within his lungs, Sal suddenly felt a wire encircling his bull neck. He knew instantly what it was—a garrotte made of piano wire—and he tried vainly to pull his head back into the car while fumbling to get his hands free from their present entanglement in the seatbelt shoulder straps.

Like a cheese cutter, the wire quickly disappeared within the fleshy part of his neck while blood spurted in all directions, within moments cutting right through his trachea and the large blood vessels in his neck. Soon thereafter, the driver's enormous head slammed against the partially opened window in one last futile attempt to free himself, shattering the exposed glass into numerous shards with one impaled into his left eyeball.

Once the man breathed his last agonizing breath, Sasha removed his bloodstained windbreaker, turned it inside out and ran quickly into a building on the opposite side of the street. Making his way expeditiously to the roof by way of the service elevator, he made a beeline to the corner area where his duffel bag lay. Extracting his state of-the-art sniper rifle, he adroitly positioned himself to execute his target as soon as he exited the revolving doors of the building. Allowing him to approach the car before shooting would be a grave mistake, as any possibility that he'd spot his driver's bloody, lifeless corpse would cause him to flee the scene. Besides, he loved utilizing his new weapon. There was something so magical about watching a cranium explode from a sniper's perfectly targeted projectile.

Within a few minutes Dominic emerged, briefcase and deployed umbrella in hand, partially obscuring his face. No matter, it'd be fun going for a head shot nevertheless, extrapolating its precise location in his mind. Sasha counted to six, controlled his breathing, and then discharged a round. The successful entrepreneur, racketeer, and family man ceased to exist in this world, his body collapsing in a heap with his face completely obscured, the umbrella's nylon material having nestled on top of his torso and head.

It wouldn't take long for the people who rushed to help the stricken man to scream in horror when they discovered his shattered, partially empty skull.

***

Scott discovered that the Brighton Beach mafia group with its newly appointed *Pakhan*, Sasha Makedonsky, was to conduct a *skhodki*— meeting—in the trendy Kashkar Café, where he conveniently installed the newest SPYTEL-M surveillance camera, along with a covert listening device.

Sasha reveled in his new role as *avtoritety*.

"My friends," Sasha said with his heavily accented English, "I've been coming up to speed with the number and scope of our businesses, some legitimate, others more in the line with what suits us. We gave many *rubles* to certain Brooklyn charities, which was fine, but we need not lose focus on our bread and butter. Please refer to the paper in front of you." He was always mindful of hidden bugging devices.

Money-laundering, computer hacking, ransom attacks, drugs, the health industry, and so forth...

He'd also listed additional activities such as money earned from 'protective' services, that almost every business in that part of Brooklyn was forced to pay or suffer the consequences.

***

"Lauren, there's no simple way to say this, so I'm going to just come out with it. Our lives are in danger." Dante sat back, relieved that the words were out of his mouth, though worried about how she'd take such disturbing news.

Lauren's big saucer-like eyes registered surprise and incredulity, though not completely.

"What... What're you saying?"

"Hear me out. Ever since I was promoted to the damn CEO position, my life's been a living hell, to be perfectly honest. First, these criminal types come to me to let me know that they thwarted a blackmail scheme. That is, some group of would-be 'businessmen' had ingeniously assembled a bunch of downtrodden guys to participate in a scheme to pretend to have certain serious diseases, with forged medical records to corroborate, get them treated, and then sue the doctors and hospitals for failing to recognize these Munchausens, fake patients with made-up stories, beforehand. So, this man then marches into my office after I myself had treated such an individual and subsequently named in a malpractice lawsuit, informing me that the 'problem' had been eliminated."

"How so?" Lauren inquired, who'd been made aware of only a part of the story.

"I don't know, and frankly at the time, didn't want to know. I then told him that I was the last person who'd cower to a blackmail scheme."

"To curry favor?"

"Exactly. I then find out that he aided and abetted several big 'admitter' physicians to my hospital to defraud the insurers, our hospital, and essentially operate their practices like they were printing money, a sizeable cut earmarked for their organization." Dan took more than a sip of scotch before continuing. "That was just a minute piece of a much larger criminal enterprise. They then forced me off the road while driving at night, another 'love tap' to warn me to get in line. You see, I essentially riled up their business partners. Then there was the ransomware attack, which threatened patient safety and could've put our beloved hospital out of business, the loss of revenue in the millions."

Dan held his arms out as if to say, "Can you believe these guys?"

"Lastly your poisoning, Lauren, when they mistakenly believed you were my girlfriend. All to get me to play ball with their extortion and racketeering plans and general assault on our healthcare industry as we know it."

Lauren stared at Dan in stony silence. It was all so overwhelming.

"There'd more. These past few months, after I treated Dominic Antonetti, I've been informed that he became so grateful that he tried to redirect the threats. The Russian mafia of Brighton Beach, their leaders learning of this change of heart and who'd poisoned him with arsenic as a warning, decided to make him a dead man walking."

Lauren gasped. "I've been involved in litigation with this man."

"Oh?"

"He's very devious and dangerous. I was told that as the Italian mafia declined in influence, Antonetti had decided strategically to align his family with the Russian mafia, who were on the ascendency." Lauren repositioned herself in her chair, her anxiety level now through the roof.

"Yeah, change of tactics. The Russian mob likes to emulate Putin's methods on occasion. Their reputation's that of extreme violence. They're crazy bastards, I'm told. That's why enough is enough."

Lauren buried her head in her hands. "This is so very much to comprehend, Dan. Really difficult to fathom. Can't we go to the police?"

"We can do so, sure, but even they can't protect us 24/7."

This truth remained undeniable. Their lives were in definite jeopardy.

CHAPTER SEVENTY-FOUR

Lauren peered out of the bay window in her condominium and stared at the bizarre configuration of an oak tree that had become a source of much amazement. This oak had grown horizontally, parallel to the ground, but only one foot above it. Apparently, when a young sapling it had become uprooted, fell flat but miraculously continued growing and thriving. Its roots had taken hold in the soil while its branches grew skyward, not merely surviving but flourishing. A metaphor for her life? She hoped so.

Now Dan considered a retreat, a redirection in his life, but this decision wasn't contemplated in a vacuum. Lauren had been assaulted in an attempt once again to get Dan, apparently, to do their bidding. This to allow their despicable enterprise to flourish, to expand, and usurp another healthcare institution in its place.

When, just when, would all this madness stop?

***

Dan stared at the banner headline, "Appeal for physicians of every subspecialty, particularly primary care and general surgeons, to participate in Project Medishare located in Port-Au-Prince, Haiti, the scene of yet another destructive earthquake.

He read on: "Project Medishare was created in 1994 to improve healthcare in Haiti. Since then, it has been committed to help its Haitian partners by establishing and funding sustainable programs, providing technology and equipment to hospitals, clinics, and other affiliated programs and training of Haitian physicians, nurses, and allied health professionals."

"On January 12, 2010, when Haiti was struck by a hugely destructive earthquake, a Dr. Green, along with a team of 11 doctors, was the first to arrive to help. In less than 24 hours, a critical care hospital and 300 trauma beds were set up in Port-Au-Prince by Project Medishare at the request of the Haitian President. By June 2010, the organization had treated more than 30,000 earthquake victims."

"After that earthquake, the organization expanded by building a tent hospital like a MASH unit. The field hospital then created is, as of today, one of the largest functioning urgent care hospitals in the country. The hospital has an emergency room, an intensive care unit, an operating room, and a pediatrics unit. It also has inpatient and outpatient operations that became available for future catastrophic events."

Marchetti sensed that this random Google article had reached him, or more accurately, been directed his way, for a good reason. A moment of serious doubt as to the direction his life's work had taken was being played out. The primary goal in life is not pleasure. Furthermore, we must never forget that we may also find meaning in life especially when confronted with a situation that seemed hopeless or can't be changed. Then one is challenged to change oneself.

***

Scott's ears pricked up when he overheard the issue of revenge needing to be visited upon those bastards from New Jersey. "A cokehead, Mr. Scott Mason, and Dr. Dante Marchetti, our holier-than-thou physician. Thinks he walks on water." Scott was bemused at the mention of his name along with his past addiction, but Marchetti, his father, was another matter altogether.

"Marchetti quit his job and plans imminently to escape to Haiti on some fuckin' relief mission. I'll personally fly there to kill that motherfucker."

Sasha, if nothing else, embodied the true ruthlessness of the *vory*, men of whom even a New York mafia boss once remarked, "We Italians will kill you. But the Russians are crazy—they'll kill your whole family."

CHAPTER SEVENTY-FIVE

Haiti had been devastated by several severe earthquakes, the most recent a 7.2 on the Richter scale. An event of this magnitude in such a vulnerable country was enough to pancake homes in a flash, trapping and killing innocent people inside where they slept. The human suffering in those tents was just what Dan Marchetti needed to take his mind off the threatening events that followed his promotion to the CEO role that came to be identified with his previous life. A life that years before witnessed the "trial by fire" that threatened to put him behind bars for crimes he didn't commit back as a promising intern.

"Robert Samuels, call me Bob. This should be interesting, don't you think?" The rotund family physician from Miami with the silver hair and full beard offered, extending his hand.

"Dan," Marchetti nodded affirmatively, not really wanting anyone to know his last name. Though he felt safe and unrecognized in this troubled area, he needed to proceed cautiously now and into the near future, even if he was certain the Russian mafia had better things to do than go after a man who no longer was able to impede them.

Of course, he had no knowledge of Scott Mason's killing rampage or the meaning behind the tattoo that adorned the back of Sasha's right hand, OMYT.

"It's hard to get away from me."

CHAPTER SEVENTY-SIX

Sasha didn't take long to spot the good doctor, who wasn't difficult to recognize. Numerous photos were available online for an individual in such an elevated public position. Even from 1200 meters, the slight gap between his two front teeth and the hearing aid in his left ear could be made out clearly. Details like this mattered, as Sasha noted that all the physicians there paced around in green scrubs. The temperature in Port-au-Prince, especially during the day, could be brutal. Some even walked around in long sleeves that he figured were coated with mosquito repellent. He was advised to do the same but, hell, he wouldn't be there long enough to worry about malaria, he figured. In fact, one kill shot to the head, and it would be back to the Jeep that drove him there from neighboring Dominican Republic.

To his left, on an adjoining hilltop, Scott balanced his Lobaev sniper rifle with its five-shot detachable box magazine on a wooden crate lying around, undoubtedly having once contained some country's contribution earmarked for disaster relief. However, there also were no doubt a sizeable number of goods were now being sold on the open market, as Haiti was as corrupt a country as any.

"That's him, Dr. Dan-te Mar-chetti," Sasha proclaimed under his breath, his thick Russian accent punctuating the air. He made a fist with his left hand and stuck his thumb out between his index and middle finger. A special gesture called the *figa,* meant as a derogatory symbol in his culture.

Marchetti had exited the medical tent to take one of the boxed ready meals donated by the US Army. They were stacked one on top of each other by the entrance, encased in slim brown cartons the size of a giant Cracker Jack container. The food contained within a large brown plastic packet, once activated, offered up a hot, tasty meal like a beef stroganoff or a pasta primavera. Taking his meal to a picnic table that had been set up about fifty yards from the tents, Dan eagerly shoveled a plastic spoonful of the now piping hot food into his mouth. No deafening sound from the gun's discharge was heard from that distance, but Dan's anguished cry broke the constant din of volunteers moving back and forth in the little village.

"Oh God, what?" He cried out, collapsing in a heap on the hard ground, now instinctively though gingerly feeling around on the right side of his chest where he'd felt the sudden thump. The sticky sensation of blood he was so familiar with was apparent; this, however, being his own.

Sasha waited a few minutes more before packing up his gear to dash off for the return trip back to his chartered flight out of the DR later that night. No need to hang around—his target wouldn't be expected to survive the gaping hole he put in his right thorax area. Dr. Dante Marchetti, he was sure, had been fatally wounded.

The newly appointed *Pakhan* looked up just in time to receive the tomahawk sent his way by former Seal Team Six specialist Scott Mason, the assassin responsible for obliterating a large segment of his Brighton Beach mafia group. It penetrated his forehead so deeply that it threatened to split his brain into two halves. Of course, "Sasha the Terrible," as many in law enforcement called him, was dead instantly. It proved to be the shortest of reigns for this very violent man.

***

Scott moved quickly to exit the kill zone and de-assemble his equipment before embarking on his way down to the medical village, cursing the fact that he'd been a tragic hairbreadth away from preventing the shooting. Finding his target had been straightforward with his tracking device but getting into position to take him out had been problematic.

After making his way down a rocky embankment, he managed to blend in with the throng of nurses and physicians now surrounding his father. He saw that the wound was a serious one, but hopefully, not fatal.

"Let's get him immediately to the surgical suite. Gonna need to secure all the lines in him there and prep for surgery. The right lung looks macerated and collapsed," Dr. Sam Feldstein commented, the first surgeon to come by. Feldstein, a highly experienced trauma surgeon from South Florida, was no stranger to sniper wounds, having done a tour in Afghanistan for the Army a few years after 9/11. Affable by nature but deadly serious when applying his craft, he was aware full well that every minute was crucial to affecting a more sanguine outcome for this traumatized physician. The sooner his patient became prepped and opened, the better.

By now, they'd slapped a venti-mask on Dan's face and a stretcher was brought out to transport him the fifty meters or so.

"How bad is it?" Scott overheard Dan's weakened voice inquire of his colleagues.

"Damage to right lung, looks like bleeding is moderate, taking you to the OR, Dan."

Marchetti nodded wanly, any movement supremely difficult and excruciatingly painful.

"What about police protection while we operate? After all, the shooter's still around and probably has seen that he's survived, at least for now," shouted another general surgeon, Dr. Max Rosen.

"You don't have to worry about that. The sniper's been neutralized," Scott replied.

Rosen stared at him momentarily and quizzically before returning to his critical patient and the surgery he desperately needed. Any further inquiry would have to wait for later, though each member of the entourage had had their curiosity piqued sufficiently by Scott's surprising comment.

This would be nothing short of a fight for this unfortunate doctor's life.

CHAPTER SEVENTY-SEVEN

Four days had elapsed, with the physicians cautiously optimistic about his recovery. Marchetti had required eight units of blood, removal of part of his lung, and an indwelling chest tube to help keep expanded the remainder of his right lung. Scott had taken the liberty to phone his sister, who flew out to join them. They slept in a pitched tent on the grounds, and to make themselves useful while Dan slept, they helped unload and unpack supplies that continued to arrive from countries around the world.

Now they sat on stools pulled from elsewhere in the large, tented area to huddle right next to their father's side.

"Dan, you're going to do just fine. When you're strong enough, we're going to bring you back home on one of those medivac planes," Lauren advised.

Dan listened and mouthed *thank you*, as talking seemed beyond his capability. This despite having had the endotracheal tube removed earlier, though his throat remained inflamed, worse in intensity than a strep throat he'd suffered through as a child.

"Dan, the man who did this is dead. One of the Brighton Beach mafia group," Scott whispered.

Dan's eyes widened, a knowing look now appearing on his distressed and markedly pale face.

"Scott and I have something important to disclose to you that'll come as quite a shock to you, we're afraid." Lauren stiffened and shifted her position while Scott maintained a stoic expression.

Marchetti moved to reassure her, raising his left hand slowly to hold hers, but he looked perplexed.

"We are your children."

There, it was done. The timing seemed so right.

Dan froze as if he'd received 120 volts from a faulty plug. He lowered his chin slightly in disbelief at what she was asserting but managed, "My children? The DNA I checked…"

"You suspected?"

"Yes. The DNA didn't match." The words understandable despite a severely hoarse voice.

"Well, I did also, mine was negative as well but…"

Scott found his voice, interjecting, "Mine was performed after yours, I guess, it was a positive match. It's called a chimeric result, rare but can be seen in twins, or I suspect in triplets here, since we both survived. You've heard of this rare phenomenon?"

Dan tilted his head, confused, while tears appeared at the corner of his eyes. "I believe so."

Scott read from his notes, knowing his physician father would need the exact definition: "Chimera is essentially a single organism that's made up of cells from two or more 'individuals'—that is, it contains two sets of DNA. People with chimerism rarely show visible signs of their condition. A few may have two different colored eyes, two different skin tones, patches of different colored or textured hair, and so forth…" With that, Scott held up the 23 and Me report so Dan could peruse it once his son handed him his reading glasses.

"I knew weeks ago but was fearful of saying anything," Lauren added. A pregnant pause ensued.

Finally, Dan motioned for a pad as it proved too painful to speak. He wrote:

I never gave up hope in finding you guys after your aunt took you away when you were three years old. Do you have any recollection of spending time with me? You had different names back then, Jake and Susie.

Lauren and Scott stared at each other with looks of consternation on their surprised faces. They both shook their befuddled heads, completely in the dark about this surprise.

Dan whispered, "Yes, you both were the joys of my life until I was falsely accused of those murders at Deerwood Hospital. I was exonerated when the real murderers were uncovered. Your aunt fled before I was found innocent. She thought that I was guilty as charged. Can't say that I blamed her, for it looked bleak for a while."

"Oh my God!" Lauren exclaimed.

CHAPTER SEVENTY-EIGHT

Days went by slowly, as is the case when one's in severe pain. Dan regained some of his strength each day. One afternoon, they determined that he could fly back to the States on a regular charter flight. He no longer required the assistance as offered on a Medivac airplane. Accompanying him were his two grown children, still reveling in the fact that their father's parental status had been confirmed.

"Your involvement in our lives now offers great comfort Dad—Dan. What shall we call you?" Lauren asked mischievously.

"Dan's fine. You were saying?"

"The feeling of not being wanted, as irrational as it may seem, never goes away and is the number-one lifetime issue most orphans or adoptees have to wrestle with." Lauren laughed, embarrassed, "Do you believe it? I'm a grown woman who sounds incredibly juvenile." She hesitated to collect herself, and Dan took over.

"Now that the truth's been uncovered, know this—I cherish the idea that we'll always have each other. Frankly, even though I've managed to garner several awards and prestigious positions, I've always dealt with a sense of loneliness that I carried with me, a dispiriting sensation coursing through me, I have to say. That is, until now."

Scott shook his head in agreement, and with that, they all hugged fiercely, determined to always stay connected. Just then, one of the young Haitian children with cerebral palsy who'd sustained several lacerations from the earthquake and its aftermath, approached the three slowly yet determinedly, her legs in braces and using a walker. The smile on her unbowed, radiant face would elevate any person's spirit, and as she approached Lauren, she held out her arms to the young woman.

"Hello darling, I mean, *bonjour, cherie,*" Lauren offered in return as they hugged.

A nurse who followed behind whispered, "She lost her entire family when their home collapsed. We call her a miracle child, *l'enfant miracle.*"

Watching this marvelous six-year-old trying to walk would melt the coldest of hearts but for Lauren, it was love at first sight. They all agreed on the spot that all three would stay in Haiti indefinitely, as there was so much work and help needed.

Lauren didn't know it just then, but she'd bond heavily and resolutely with the delightful child, Romilly.

EPILOGUE

Seated at a beat-up wooden picnic bench located fifty feet from the entrance to the tent earmarked for patient triage, Dan couldn't help noticing a rather well-dressed man in a blue blazer, tan khaki pants, and an open-necked white shirt engaged in conversation with one of the surgeons who enjoyed a smoke not far from where he picked at his early lunch. The appetite hadn't yet returned since his emergency surgery, his weight down a good fifteen pounds. The gentleman clearly was a visitor and overdressed to say the least. The temperature was a balmy ninety-two degrees, even at 11 in the morning. Dan observed the general surgeon, whose name escaped him, pointing in his direction, much to his surprise.

"Dr. Marchetti, just the man I came to see. Anthony Cannizzaro from the Sacred Heart Hospital. New Chairman of the Board."

"Mr. Cannizzaro, you travelled all the way down to Haiti to see me?" Dan's face was a mixture of shock and puzzlement.

"I did, Dan, and please call me Tony."

"Why have you come here, may I ask?"

"Very simply, the Board at Sacred Heart wants you back as CEO and President…"

"No, no, no," Dan vehemently interrupted him. "Never again."

"Please, Dan, hear me out, and if you're not persuaded then fine, I'll go on my way. Will you at least give me a tour of this marvelous facility so I can understand what you and your group have accomplished down here?"

"Sure thing, let me do that now." With that, they spent the next hour touring the facility, Cannizzaro shocked at how complete and ingenious the setup was considering their location in one of the poorest countries in the world.

"I feel at peace here, Tony. The people really need me and are so appreciative, you know," he offered earnestly.

At that point, Cannizzaro turned to face Marchetti, and placed both hands on his broad shoulders.

"In the six months since you left, I can plainly see that you've found a home here in Port-au-Prince performing lifesaving medical work. Admirable, for certain, but I'd be remiss if I didn't remind you that our hospital—your hospital—has no less than twenty-five percent indigent patients, who depend on the facility for all of their medical care. You were a vital cog there for many years, whose best work we all feel is still ahead of you."

Suddenly, Cannizzaro, the newly installed Chairman of the Board of Sacred Heart Hospital, with a quivering voice and glistening eyes made an observation that touched Dan Marchetti to his very core.

"Dan, those of us who stayed have been challenged to instill a different culture, one with integrity, mission-oriented, cognizant of the 'no money, no mission' mantra, but making certain that the patient's welfare is ALWAYS placed above all else. May sound Pollyanna-ish, but we're trying with everything we have to accomplish this. Be part of that, Dan. Come back and finish what you started. I promise you'll feel ultimately rewarded for doing so."

Dan stood motionless because this man seemed to know that his abandoning the hospital somewhat high and dry never totally sat well with him.

"Mr. Cannizzaro, I promise you that I'll give it a great deal of serious thought."

***

"A penny for your thoughts, Dan," Lauren said to her father as he sat atop a picnic table looking at the sun rising on another day in Port-au-Prince. A piping hot cup of coffee in his left hand threatened to scald him unless he paid more attention to it. "Either drink some or put the damn thing down, you're making me nervous."

Dan's trance now broken, he laughed and obliged by taking two prolonged sips.

"Where were you, sir?" Lauren persevered, placing her head on his shoulder while grabbing his free hand.

"Oh, looking back over my life. Plato once defined man as 'a being in search of meaning.'"

"Tell me about your search."

"You have a few hours?" He asked rhetorically. "You know, being brought up Roman Catholic, we talk constantly about the afterlife, which really when you think about it, detracts or postpones the question of one's life purpose."

"Never thought of it that way."

"The fact is that our life may not have been created with any predetermined purpose, though that does not mean it cannot have one. We can be the authors of our own purpose." Marchetti turned to face his daughter, who was now joined by Scott who'd sauntered by a few minutes before, listening intently to the conversation.

"You know I used to fancy myself somewhat of a wine connoisseur."

"I didn't know that our father was a wine sommelier," Scott interjected.

"I remember visiting the vineyards of Chateauneuf-du-Pape, where I noticed there were numerous smooth stones on the grounds. They were there, I was told, to capture the heat of the sun and release it back to the cool of the night, helping the grapes to ripen. Now, it stands to reason that these stones were not created with this purpose in mind. Even if they had been created for that reason, it would almost certainly not have been to make great wine or even to serve as bookends."

"Understood."

"Anyway, I've concluded that only certain actions and relationships that we consider valuable give life its meaning. Having rediscovered you guys has completed the circle for me. And of course, the little one, Romilly."

"Yes, the little one," Lauren agreed. Bending over to pick her up, aluminum crutches now dangling by her side, she gently hugged the "miracle child" to her chest, her high-pitched giggle a stark reminder that, despite her physical challenge, life was good.

"Lauren and Scott, I want to go home. I need to finish what I started at Sacred Heart Hospital, but I don't want to leave you behind."

"We won't let that happen, Dad." All three hugged tightly, afraid to let go.

A moment later, Marchetti undid the band of his wristwatch and held it aloft.

"Look here—you see that symbol on the face of my watch, a gift I received from my parents many years ago?" Dan held it up for both Scott and Lauren to view.

"The caduceus," Lauren volunteered.

"That's correct. Lot of controversy with it."

"Why's that?" Scott inquired.

"The short staff was carried by Hermes in Greek mythology. It's entwined with two snakes and surmounted by two wings. Now, Hermes was the God of Commerce as well as the protector of thieves and conmen. This's why many healthcare professionals object to the use of this symbol." Dan paused to contemplate his next words. "On the other hand, the snake in many cultures was used to symbolize emotions characterized by tremendous respect. So, you see, while many consider the caduceus to be a false symbol for medicine, it's not necessarily so. It's a matter of one's perspective. You can guess where I stand." He continued, "Supporting patients from various backgrounds on their recovery journeys… An honor when people are at their lowest, most vulnerable point in life. Particularly observing them gradually improve. There remains no better experience. I feel needed in so many ways and abundantly blessed."

THE END